THE MATCH GIRL

BEATRICE WYNN

CHAPTER 1

hitechapel was a lot noisier, the air floating with the neighs of hungry horses, clanking carriage wheels, and the loud giggles of the silk-clad ladies out for their evening walks. Far ahead, Mary watched as five men clung to the rear rail of a crowded omnibus as it lurched down road. She breathed out a little scoff.

Risking their lives, those lads.

Like always, she settled with bothering about her realest concerns, the matchboxes she was to sell. She needed good food, and maybe some new shoes. Her boots, too thin for the cold slapped through puddles dark with soot and something worse, and every breath she took was thick with coal dust and the day's rain.

Sighing, she rattled a matchbox in her hand, glad that it was near empty. One more hour, she told herself. One more hour and maybe she'd have enough for bread…or a corner by the baker's grate. Behind her, the city murmured and moaned, its secrets tucked behind railings, within alleyways, beneath the theatre ruins where even ghosts had gone quiet.

"We must hurry!"

She watched the lady in silk flag down a cab, her face squeezed with aggravation. With hardly a pause, the other pedestrians followed suit, their fast paces cooking up a little clamour. Even the gaslights seemed to be growing dimmer, throwing the streets further and further into a shadowy bubble.

Mary slapped away an unruly curl of hair from her face. What in heaven's name was going on?

She was just going to take a step forward when she heard the mountain-splitting sound.

She froze, right there in the middle of the alleyway, her heart pounding in fury set alight by her grumbling belly. Did those blood-hungry blokes not know when to stop? The rain had fallen incessantly all day, stealing all the time she could have harnessed in selling a dozen more matchboxes. And now, there had to be another encumbrance?

God help her if the slam-bang thundering were indeed gunshots. Because indeed, if some folks somewhere had become touched in the head, they'd have to suffer the harshest possible recompense! She tucked her wares back into her reticule, her cold feet slamming against the cracked cobblestones.

"Mister, I must talk to you!" She waved at the constables just by the pavement railing, struggling hard to keep her discontentment at bay. People were running about for their dear lives and they just stood there, cracking wanton and dry jokes? Their customary slackness she was used to, but at this critical hour, she'd make sure to be the catalyst for change.

"Are your ears blocked to the noise?" The one with a bald head took the front, his eyes weighing her down in a nasty way. "Hurry home. I do not want to have to deal with the corpse of a costermonger."

"I cannot hurry home." She took a step closer, her nose squeezing in response to the smoke pouring off their pipes. "I believe the uproar is from two streets downtown. If we hurry, we'll catch the culprits."

The constables gave off the loudest and most irritating guffaw she'd ever heard, the sardonic glaze over their eyes growing thicker. She clenched her fists, wishing she could use it on the one with the squared jaw and ugly dimples.

"Go home already," the bald-headed man repeated; his tone more dismissive than before. "If I have to repeat to you the same words, I promise you won't like the consequences."

She had been around long enough to know he was dead-core serious. He was the most brutal of them, more towards the street urchins trying to make a decent living than towards the criminals who actually deserved the brutality. She looked back at the streets. Asides from a couple other men who had developed a thick skin towards the war that daily broke out in the area, everyone else had long fled for their lives.

"Hey match girl, you've got one of those boxes you carry around?"

Her heart leaped. "You give me a penny, I give you a box." One of the constables was setting the offer, but she didn't mind who her buyer was, as long as it fetched her a couple coins for bread. Already, the ache in her belly was growing louder than the church bells echoing from St. Giles.

The constable touched his pistol, his eyes glittering with unspoken evil. "A box. Now!"

She deduced his intent only a heartbeat later.

Usually, her only form of defence against such bad thieving men were the witnesses scattered across the sunny and busy streets of London. However now, with the shadows stretching and the streets whispering, such benefits stood no ground.

In other words, she was ruined.

Her Ma used to call this time of the night the *ghost hour*. Though dead for six winters now, she'd say the shadows weren't the ones to be feared. The men who didn't speak were crueller, the ones with polished boots and blood under their fingernails. Like this Constable here.

Force would clearly not work with him. She took a small step forward, trying to buy some time, her head scouring desperately for some plan that'd end with food in her belly.

"A box definitely is no issue, sire." She gulped some spittle down her dry throat. "The only knots to be untied now are those in my belly." Her voice quivered, enough to ignite empathy in them if their hearts weren't already frozen. "If you'd only give me a penny, I'll be able to afford a meal to save my growling..."

Another gunshot reverberated through the air, stealing the words off her lips and setting her heart in a wild dance.

The constable with the bald head looked off, in the direction the sounds came from, his face coloured with an irritation she knew would get him moving. *Good.* He shot a glare at the thieving constable. "What's a penny to you? Give the girl and stop the trouble." He grabbed his baton from the wooden bench close to him and blew through the whistle dangling from a rope around his neck. "We've got to get things in order down there before the Commissioner gets us throttled."

Oh perfect, perfect.

She plucked a matchbox from her reticule, unable to rid the rhapsodic look off her face. The thieving constable clearly was infuriated, his jaws taut and his chest heaving like a mad bull's. He tossed the coin at her, the shiny piece flying through the air and then, falling in the mud, a few inches from where she stood.

What was a little dirt to someone at hunger's mercy?

"That nipper's got more dirt than shoes on."

It didn't matter whoever it was that muttered the words. She picked the coin even more heartily and pressed the box into his widespread palm. "Thank you, Mister."

He didn't look happy a bit. "It's a small town," he

whispered, his voice a force through gritted teeth. "I'll get you, surely."

She nodded exuberantly, like she'd not just heard him whisper some ugly threats into her ear. "I'm off now, Constables! Good luck catching those bas..."She hurriedly cleared her throat. "Those…huh…criminals. "She gave them a small wave and began to make her way back.

"Not so fast, girl."

She stopped in her tracks, spinning on her feet almost immediately. *Was someone else going to buy a match box?* Her heart managed another leap. That'd be the greatest sales ever to be made on a night as stormy as this!

The bald-headed man took two big steps towards her, his huge figure easily towering her. "The other time…" He eyed her under his thick lashes briefly, like she was some criminal he was set to investigate. "You spoke like you were very informed of the happenings down there."

"I spoke?" She stuttered, now recalling the very foolish words she'd uttered, all in the sake of the hunger that'd stabbed her belly.

He narrowed his eyes at her until they looked like small slits that led to deep black wells. "Two streets downtown…" He trailed off, like his words were the very keys that'd stir up her memory. "You mentioned that the other time."

She gave off a shaky laugh. "Ah, pardon me, Mister, but I certainly must have forgotten my place." She pulled off a look that fully defined *surpr*ise. "How could I know anything of the evils that happen in this town?" She took a small step backward. "I'm just an ignoramus trying to sell matchboxes to survive. Now, if you'll just overlook my slips, I promise to never again get in your way."

"She's coming with us." The thieving constable's voice was alight with revenge. He smirked at her, his left hand clutching the barrel of his gun in a not so friendly way.

Mouth dry, she looked away. "I must find food now, for my legs have become weak..."

"Lead the way!"

So booming was the bald headed man's voice that the penny she'd just gained fell back into the mud. She hurriedly picked it up and tucked it safely into her side pocket, hoping in heaven's sake that she survived whatever was about to befall her.

Perhaps, in her next life, she'd learn the art of due reticence. Horrified, she pulled her cloak tighter around me, the cold breeze stinging her through the thin fabric. "This way," She murmured, before quietly turning around and leading the way, down the walks and into the deserted roads.

Whitechapel was the house of every criminal in London—hardened men and felons that had murdered and slaughtered men like they were cows, thieves that ran the streets with guns and blades tucked into their boots, and drug barons that were always red in the face.

And now, she was the one leading the Police to them. Innocent she. The thought almost made her laugh at herself, only that she was in some hot and dire situation that decapitated such possibilities.

A carriage ran down the street just then, and she managed to catch a girl her age inside, laughing. Herbold front wilted into nothing. Perhaps, she could tell just how foolish she was.

She took a turn down the corner, and then, another, the footsteps of the Constables loud in her ears. It didn't even help that she couldn't hear whatever things they were saying. Only one thing was sure. If they were whispering, it meant that she was to be used as bait.

Goodness gracious.

The farther they moved; the more certain she became of the evil undertones to their quiet discussions. She slowed to a stop at the famous marsh garden, a plan materializing in her head.

"I'm afraid I cannot go further."

"You must want a bullet in your head."

She'd recognize the voice of the thieving Constable in a beat. "My body calls for ease…" She rubbed her clammy palms against the fabric of her dress. "…in certain ways I'll be too shamefaced to describe."

"What's she rambling on about?" the one with the ugly dimple asked.

"I'm a lady, Constables and I have to..." She gritted her teeth. "Must I need be explicit?"

"A second!"

She beamed at the bald-headed man. "Certainly, sire." She dived into the tall guinea just within the shadows, her legs barely resting on the ground for a second.

"I think she's fleeing!"

There again, the voice of the thieving Constable. Even if they tried to set off after her, they'd only get lost in the woods. She knew every nook and cranny of the town. All they had were ridiculous maps that'd only get them more confused.

She was going to cross the stream when she heard it—a muffled cry, raw and broken, just past the barrels behind the fishmonger's stall. She froze. Most girls would have run. But having survived on instinct, she made a dive for it, her curiosity getting the better of her.

She rounded the corner and almost stumbled.

A boy—no, a man—lay crumpled in the gutter. His shirt was soaked dark, and his lip was split so wide she could see the gleam of teeth. She stared at him, wide-eyed. One arm was twisted beneath him, and there was blood. So much blood.

"Oi," She whispered, kneeling. "You alive?"

His eyes fluttered, then focused. They were grey, like smoke in winter. "Help me," he rasped.

She tried to weigh her odds but his beautiful eyes set a mist in her head.

"Can you walk?" If that wasn't her making an effort to sound lady-like!

He groaned in answer, which wasn't very helpful.

If she left him, he'd die. That was the way of it in this part of London. You live or rot, and the world doesn't flinch. Besides, wasn't he such a comely man to stare at?

She pressed her palms beneath his arms. "Come on, then. You're lucky I know a place."

CHAPTER 2

The warning bells in her head wouldn't stop jingling off. Mary placed her hands on her hips and let out a shaky exhale, the puff billowing out in a plume of vapor, like steam escaping from a boiling kettle.

An almost dead guy in her arms while the echoes of gunshots filled the air? Nobody would believe her story. Not even the Constables, seeing as she'd absconded on a crafty note. They would only have her locked in the darkest of the cells, or worse still, place her in solitary confinement.

Her gaze fell on the lad again, her brain straining and stretching, all to find a reason to desert the lad.

Already, she'd dragged him a couple miles away from the gutter, courtesy of the old handcart she'd found lying just by the side. He still looked just as dead...and horrible. But her heart wouldn't stop melting, like candle to the flame. Perhaps, it had already become gooey, who knew?

"Oh Mary, get a grip!" She ground out, her eyes piercing through the dark as she scanned the fields. *No one yet.* Good.

Mustering all the strength left in her starved body, she gripped the cart's handles and dragged the boy's dead weight through the East End's filth-slick alleys. The old handcart rattled and shrieked over every cobblestone, and a couple not-so-good times, the tire would get caught in the mud, making her see red.

She hated being nervous. And it didn't help that every shift in the distance set her alight with an unhealthy dose of the nervousness. For all she knew, the folks that did wrong to the lad could still be somewhere, hovering around and plotting the evil they'd do to her.

Perhaps, they'd skin her alive, stuff her in a nylon bag and then, stitch the bag until it looked like an harmless ball of garbage.

Thousands of shivers danced their way up her spine, but she kept on pushing, stopping only when she had to wipe off the small beads of perspiration clustered at the top of her forehead.

She cut through Cutler's Lane, down behind the sandwich seller's hovel, through the split iron fence just behind it, and past the crumbling brickwork swallowed by ivy. And there, hidden behind the world's forgetting stood her theatre.

It had no name. The sign had long rotted off before she found the building. All that was left now was ruin—termite-infested wooden rails, broken windows, hollow rafters, and dust that powdered the air with her every step on the floorboards.

None of that mattered to her either way. The theatre was her sanctuary. It remembered what the world had long forgotten, and that notion alone gave solace to her lonely heart.

She slowed the cart to a stop when she arrived at the trapdoor. "You better be worth all of this, lad," she muttered, wiping the sweat off her brow with her sleeve. "You wake up as a monster and I won't hesitate to give you a beating with the Iron pan I picked off the trash."

With a strength too foreign to her, she pushed the boy to his feet and wound his good arm round her neck. Oh, the weight, the weight…Her muscles protested and her knees wobbled unsurely. Entirely exhausted, she tried to place him back in the cart, only stopping when *manly*, though weak grunt escaped his lips.

"You're alive!" She let out an excited whistle and then hurried to drag him in, her weakness long swallowed up.

Inside, the smell of damp velvet and old plaster clung to everything. Everything looked old and ready to crumble. She glanced briefly at the lad—the very first person she'd brought in in years, like she could somehow know what was running through his mind.

Perhaps, the poor boy thought he'd kicked the bucket and arrived at hell. And really, she didn't blame him. Hell perhaps was better than her place of abode.

She laid him on a threadbare curtain that she'd found at the rag store, her hands hurrying to get him straightened out and comfortable. Every move made him groan, and then, she'd reassure him like she had everything figured out.

She dug her hand into her reticule, plucked a matchbox and then, lit the candle. "See, lad, this matchstick would fetch me lunch! But I chose to help you instead. Don't forget that when you wake up!"

She settled the candle stand on the stool just close to where he lay. The flickering candlelight made him look softer. Younger. His face, though bruised and swollen at the edges still had a kind shape to it—a square jaw, lashes too long for a dock rat—

She held back the gasp that threatened to make its way past her lips. Was that admiration stirring up within her? "Oh my!" Alarmed, she took a step back, willing herself to focus!

How could she have thoughts that outrageous?

Hands trembling and heart pumping, she dampened a cloth and then began to wipe away the dried blood from his face and temple. "You are just...a lad I found in the gutter, nothing more." She threw the cloth into the bucket of water with a little more force than necessary and then wrung it into a ball.

His hot skin made her worry. He had a fever. "I don't even know your name, lad." She worked the cloth to his shoulders. "What do I do with you?"

When she finished, she rose to her feet and began to prowl about the room. He needed medication, and she was sure the Chapel would be willing to give some. Only that the matron would have her swallow the pills before leaving. The woman utterly detested waste.

She stilled to a stop. *What if his family were on the search for him?* He could be the son of a Constable for all she knew! Hastily, she sank back to her knees and worked her way through his pockets, in the hope of finding some form of identification.

She was just going to pull her hands out when her eyes caught on to something. His fists. She settled beside him, a frown knitting her brows. They were tightly clenched around something—a crumpled piece of red cloth, though slightly frayed at the edges. Curious, she pried his fingers loose.

Crimson silk. *Fancy*. She turned the material in her hand, her gaze flying about the edges. It was marked with something. She looked a little more closely, her eyes squinting.

A fist stitched in black thread?

She blinked, trying to—

A fist stitched in black thread!

The image struck a chord almost immediately, and in response, her stomach made a double flip. She knew that symbol. Everyone in the East End knew what that was. It was the *Crimson Fist!*

Horrified, she looked at the lad and back at the fabric, trying to tie the innocent look on his face to the fist. The fist represented a gang so ruthless that even the Constables had long learned to not interfere with their dealings. The leader was whispered to be a ghost. Some even spoke of how he'd light his cigars with the ribbons of match girls.

She gasped, the sound of her heart wild in her ears.

The lad she'd helped had their mark clutched in his hand. Oh goodness. She didn't even know why she wasn't already hyperventilating.

She looked at him again, her heart pounding even more strongly in her chest.

Was he one of them?

Her gaze immediately travelled to the sledgehammer she had hidden beneath one of the floorboards. Her ma had always talked about self-defence, and perhaps, now was the time she'd try that.

She exhaled, her insides wilting at the thought of hitting someone with a hammer. She gazed pointedly at the lad. "You had better not be..."

What if he had crossed them? She studied him more closely. He looked like he couldn't even kill a fly. Perhaps, the gang had done that to him.

Lightning cracked in the distance. A rat skittered across the balcony a second later, scaring her a bit. She rose to her feet and then, tucked the red scrap into her boot, determination slowly burning away the fear in her heart.

If he brought danger to her theatre, she'd have to know. However, for now, he was bleeding. And regardless of the trouble that followed, him dying was the very last on her list.

She tore strips from the hem of her old chemise and bound the worst of his wounds. At least, she'd watched the Matron at the Chapel do that when the street lads rushed in with injuries after a fight.

The fever made him mumble—nonsense words at first. Then, a clear whisper:

"Ledger…don't let them find it…"

She froze.

Ledger?

What did he mean by—

Could it be he had secrets? Perhaps, he'd seen something he shouldn't have. Her heart began to grow wild all over again. She'd dragged home more than just trouble. She'd dragged home a secret worth killing for.

She leaned back on her heels, staring down at him, unsure of what to do.

Outside, the storm broke. Rain hammered the rooftop like God himself was warning her. But no mattered how much she wanted to, she didn't run. She didn't bolt the trapdoor. She stayed.

She just stayed!

And that was mostly because under all the fear and fury in her chest, she felt something else looming. It annoyed her to admit it, but she had a very strange and sharp pull towards the broken boy.

Besides, the theatre had sheltered her for years. However, tonight….for the first time, she wasn't alone in the dark. She felt warmth and all that good furry feeling.

She was just going to find another rag she could use to keep his head elevated when a sound cut through the silence—wood groaning beneath weight…then, footsteps. She stilled immediately, all her senses hot and alert. The steps were very light and could have been excused as some scurrying rat. But she knew her home well enough, the creatures within it and the kind of sounds they let out.

That was no rat!

Someone had found their way in.

She snatched the knife she'd tucked safely at the side of her boot, every muscle in her small frame coiled like a spring. The knife was an inheritance from her Ma, but the art of using it she knew nothing about. She'd heard of stories where knives were lunged at the enemy's bellies or eyes. *She* shivered at the thought of blood pooling about her sacred floorboards—

The trapdoor creaked.

Oh God!

She hurried to blow out the candle and then waited, her breath trapped somewhere in her throat. This had never happened all through the time she'd lived alone. Whoever they were, they clearly had been attracted by the lad she'd saved.

The first footstep had her jump a little. For a moment, she'd been hoping to be wrong. She'd hoped that her mind had only played a trick on her, making her misinterpret the wind's waves for someone. But now, with actual footsteps, the little hope died, leaving her to stare breathlessly at the dark space in front of her.

She gripped the handle of the knife much tighter and then, crept towards the trapdoor, every inch of her vibrating with tension. Whoever it was, they sure weren't stumbling in by accidents. They were also not drunk.

Their steps were careful, almost calculated, like they were hunting after a prey.

She pressed herself against the wall, her heart hammering in her ears and her knife ready. Hopefully, she made the right swing and ended the horror in time. She was too hungry for all the drama.

But then, the next footstep never came.

Mouth dry, she waited, hating how the silence wrapped her like a duvet. Even her body seemed to grow silent too, leaving her unsure of what to do next.

Where did they go?

CHAPTER 3

"Kill him."

The other masked man that stood alongside the one who'd spoken pulled out a knife from the hoops of his belt, his eyes dark with loathe. He watched him struggle against the binds for a minute, a small smirk tugging at his lips. "Save your strength, you whelp." He unsheathed the knife in a move and began to advance towards him, his thick leather boots crushing the grass in its path.

Will, blinded by the blade's lustre beneath the moonlight, shut his eyes close, waiting for the final strike. His heart already had stilled, like it had somehow accepted the evil fate designated to it. Soon enough, the man was a breath away, the smell of wood and smoke pouring off his body.

Will clenched the fabric in his hand tighter, his breath held.

"Die!"

"No!"

Will woke up with a start, his heart thudding wildly like a trapped bird, desperate to escape his chest.*He could still see the knife, feel the pain.* Raw. Biting. Intense. He held his head in his hands, the ache there slicing through every angle. Even his lungs felt too small, each breath a battle against invisible weight.

Water.

He needed water.

He tried to look up, only to feel the worst pain tear across his belly.His skin prickled with goose-bumps, and his nerves jangled like loose chains.He'd been stabbed. He remembered—the relentless digging into his viscera until the breath escaped his lips.

He shut his eyes, horrified.

He had to bring his mind to focus. Whatever it was that had happened to him, he needed to know. The air carried with it the scent of damp wood, smoke, and something warm, like old paper curling in fire. His senses sprang in alert. Hadn't his killer smelled the same way?

THE MATCH GIRL

His eyes sprang open at once, blinking harshly and quickly, to get rid of the blur that had coated his vision. A wavering glow of a single candle. He squinted at it, feeling the pressure build in his eyes. Its flame danced like a moth against his eyelids, and for a razor-thin moment, he thought he was home.

Only that there was no way he could have made it home, at least not after being stabbed like a pig.

He tried to move, but his body protested every slight movement as though he'd been trampled by horses. His ribs felt like they'd been shattered and then, plastered back in place. His head throbbed with too many dark memories he couldn't even place. Everything seemed hurt, broken, and out of place.

He looked around again, his vision acclimating slowly to the darkness.

The room looked too unfamiliar, yet similar to his home—the broken pieces, the old items, the rags, everything. Anxious, he licked his lower lip; only for the taste of blood and rust to collideagainst his taste buds.

"Oh God."

He sucked in a breath. The pain flared, and he had to grit his teeth to hold back the groan in his throat. If the gang had locked him somewhere, it'd be best to not have them know he was awake. Perhaps, his body would cooperate and allow him sneak out unnoticed.

The thought however died as soon as it came. Footsteps, light and cautious made way towards him, making him grow cold, all the way down to his toes. He was helpless. There was no way he could move or hide. His body wouldn't let him.

He quickly scanned the area for some knife…or pipe he could use to defend himself. But whoever had kept him there had surely done a very clean sweep of the area. Nothing sharp or helpful lay in sight.

His eyes threatened to shut close, out of the weakness he felt, but he forced them back open, straining them with the little strength he had left.

He couldn't sleep now, at least, not with the person coming towards him.

The person flashed on a matchstick, and in a blink, the area grew brighter. And then, he saw a face, though dimly lit by the candlelight. They seemed to pause when they caught his gaze, like they were shocked to see him awake.

His heart beat the fastest at that time. He wasn't sure he could go through the ordeal of another stab. However, before he could even make move, a very feminine voice tore through his ears, holding him just in place.

"Goodness gracious!" She ran towards him and knelt beside him, her face half-lit by the candle. Her dark hair was pulled back, but a loose strand framed her cheek."You're awake!"

He blinked at her, unsure of whatever was happening. He wasn't in the custody of his killer, but a young lady? He coughed, the motion wracking his chest. How in heaven's name had she found him? How did she get him here? Who was she?

"You should not be sitting!" She tried to lifthis shirt, but he stopped her immediately, too shocked by her audacity. Ladies knew not to touch men like that, not to talk of men they didn't even know.

"Where am I?" He ground out weakly, feeling the wound burn a little more strongly. "Who are you?"

"Oi, you should not look at me like I did you wrong!" Her small dark eyes grew fiery. "If I were you, I'd be glad I was safe and hidden from the world's turbulence!"

He swallowed. "Where…am I?"This time, he ground out his words more firmly, desperate to get answers.

If the gang discovered that his body was missing,

they'd surely be on the lookout for him, and that would put her at risk.*Whoever she was.*

"Listen,your wounds are only barely dressed." Fear poured out with her words, and he couldn't even bring himself to understand why she was that concerned. "If you sit like this for longer, you'll be at risk of complications…an haemorrhage, more blood loss, fainting spells..."

"Who are you and where is this place?" His voice came on more strongly than he'd intended, and the shock in her eyes made him feel sorry for her.

But for Pete's sake, he was far from comfortable! In his books, she could be anyone!

"Knowing who I am won't change anything." She placed a hand on his forehead. "You're burning."

Her touch made him jump. Her hands; soft, cold, anddelicate, radiated too much comfort to his burning body. Uncomfortable, he slapped her hand off again. "What's this place and why did you bring me here?"

She glanced around the room for a second—broken balconies overhead, scattered tools, a rotting curtain pinned against the far wall. "This is the theatre everyone abandoned years ago." She looked into his eyes. "You probably don't remember, but that's nothing. It's safe here."

He tried again to rise, but his knees buckled beneath him, mocking him.

Her hand shot out, gripping his arm. "Easy!" she hissed.

He closed his eyes, letting the pain wash over him. Flashes of memory—his brother's face twisted in terror as the gang dragged him into the fog; the ledger, its pages damp with brine and blood; the hiss of a match lighting.

He shivered, not from cold.

"Why'd you help me?" His mouth felt like ash.

She didn't answer right away. Her eyes lingered on the bruises he didn't remember earning.

"I've seen too many left to die," she said finally. "Didn't want to see one more."

He watched her. The flickering light made her look older, but there was something fragile tucked beneath the grit—something she'd buried deep.

"You got a name?"

She hesitated, for a second. "Mary."

"Will." His voice cracked.

She nodded. "I know."

That caught him. "How?"

"You kept mumbling it when I dragged you here." She shook her head slowly, like there was something she also didn't understand. "That, and something about a ledger."

Ah. The ledger. The damned thing that might've gotten him and his brother killed. Driven by impulse, he tried to rise up again, but failed.

"Don't," she warned, this time, her voice as firm as his had been. "You've lost a lot of blood."

"You know nothing of the danger tied to what you're doing." Frustration budded with his voice, and he only hoped she heard it and let him go. "The people that put me in this condition…" He gritted his teeth, angryfor the first time since he'd processed everything. "They are dangerous people. You don't want to appear in the picture."

He waited to see the terror in her eyes, but she only stared at him calmly, her eyes intermittently accessing his wounds.

"Do you hear me? It's unsafe!"

She let out a scoff and rose to her feet. "You won't make it an inch out of here without assistance." She pulled one wobbly drawer open. "Your body won't concur, no matter how strong your wishes to leave are."

She brought out a tin and then, shut the drawer back close. "You also don't have to worry about me."

THE MATCH GIRL

In a second, she was back beside him, the tin sitting in the small space between them.

"You don't know anything!" Her insistence and calm front was now beginning to get him annoyed.

She opened the tin and brought out a piece of stale bread. "You should eat. You look ready to pass out again."

He slapped the bread away from him, causing it to fly across the room to somewhere the light didn't cover. "Don't be nice to me. Let me leave!" Every passing moment felt like hell. The gang could show up and wreck her house. They'd kill them both, surely. How then could she—

"You throw food away?" she screamed, her eyes burning with fury. The kindness that moulded her posture suddenly vanished and soon, she propped up on her knees, her gaze tearing hotly into his. "By some very strange and cursed luck, you found someone to help you, and in return for their impossible show of kindness, you throw their food away?"

He almost apologized.

She looked just ready to snap, like lightning across dark skies.

"Look, I remain indebted to you, but those people will..."

"You think I don't know what you're talking

about?" She pointed a finger at him. "When I found you, you were clutching this fabric." Her face turned the faintest pink, the exertion clear in her voice. "I saw the mark. I know who they are."

He blinked. Once, then twice.

"Come on now, cat got your tongue?"

"You don't know the people you're talking about." His words streamed as a little whisper, the fire in it doused.

She let out an humourless laugh. "You must be kidding. I don't know the Crimson Fist?" She laughed a little more. "I've lived in the slums all my life. I know them…alongside a couple other gangs just as deadly as they are."

His jaw almost dropped. How was she not terrified?

"They are after something. There's this book I had—it's important. They think I know too much." He stared into her eyes, trying hard to strike a dot of reasoning. "In their books, I cannot be alive. Anyone that's caught with me suffers the same fate as I. You get that?"

She rose to her feet and very fluidly found the bread I'd thrown away. "You're going to eat this." She knelt beside me again. "I don't appreciate waste. Bread costs a fortune now, in case you forgot."

Oh God, Oh God.

How thick skinned was she? Nothing he said, no matter how blood-curdling he made it to be, seemed to get to her.

"What happens after I eat?"

She shrugged. "We'll see. Eat first."

He collected the bread from her and bit into it in a rush. The dry crumb cracked against his teeth, but he really couldn't afford to waste any more time.

He was just about to take on the last bite when he began to choke. His lungs tightened and burned, sending his eyes rolling behind their sockets.

"Being obstinate does no good." She arrived with a cup of water. "You should know that."

He gulped the water greedily, desperate for a grip on air. At some point, she began to pat his back gently, but he couldn't have minded any less, at least, not when he was struggling to breathe.

He only felt better a couple of minutes later, and he made sure to avoid her eyes, embarrassed. "I don't understand why you're helping me."

"You'd have done the same for me." She pulled back, scanning my wounds. "You lost a lot of blood."

"How do you know that?"

She looked at me. "Know what?"

"That I'd have done the same?" He forced a bitter

laugh to his lips. "I could be just as evil as them. You cannot be so sure."

"I read people for a living. If I'd thought otherwise of your tendencies, I'd have long thrown you out of my house."

The solidness with which she spoke relaxed him a little. "They wanted the ledger back." His voice came as a rasp.

Her eyes flickered—fear? Understanding? "They'll come looking."

He felt his chest tighten, the memories all pouring in again. "I saw him," he let out, in a whisper. "Black Crow. He wore a serpent tattoo on his wrist. He asked if I knew my brother's name."

A hard edge crept Into her features. "Then they know who you are."

She stood up, grabbed a towel and a bowl of water, and crouched at my side like before. "I'll need to take down your temperature."

He didn't respond. His thoughts were long settled on the evil that had befallen him.

Silence settled between them, broken only by the candle's sputter. His mind raced: how deep did this go? Who in London's murky depths would kill to keep the ledger secret? And what did it truly contain?

She returned and sponged his head, shoulders and arm gently, bringing him back to a present time filled with her scent. She smelled like sunshine on old linens—warm, clean, and oddly comforting. She was beautiful, with a cute button nose that wrinkled as she worked.

He sighed, choosing instead to focus on the room. He be damned to let his thoughts wander any farther. There were old posters peeling from the walls, and above them, the ghostly outline of the stage arch. The theatre seemed to breathe, its silence heavy with memories of laughter and tears.

"You know," She dumped the towel in the bowl. "Before you think of escaping, it'd be good for you to know that something…" She let out a shaky breath. "Something funny happened before you came around."

His heart picked up on its race. "What's that?"

She sat straighter. "I think someone has been watching this place." She raked her hands through her hair. "I felt it last night. Heard footsteps, tried to find out who they were."

Cold spread through his body, and it had nothing to do with the room."You saw someone?" He shifted closer to her. "What did they look like?"

She nodded. "No, justfootsteps…just like I'm hearing now, again."

They both stilled at once, and listened. Will could feel his skin prickle. At first, he heard nothing but the slow drip of water and their rough breathing. But a split second later, his ears drew in the sound.

Faint. Measured.

A board creaking above.

Mary moved without a word. Snuffed the candle. Drew her knife.

He lay frozen, eyes wide in the dark. His heart beat a panicked rhythm in his throat. *Had they found him?*

Then came the light.

A single flare of orange.

Someone had struck a match above the trapdoor.

Mary didn't breathe. Neither did he.

The ember flared for just a second, then vanished into fog.

In the dark, across the room, he caught her gaze.

Someone was near. And they didn't know who they were.

CHAPTER 4

The last time she didn't get any sleep at night was when her Ma died. She'd cried a river, her dreams haunted endlessly by the most horrendous of figures.It'd been a horrible feeling, losing the one woman she loved, to death's cold arms. And every night, she'd prayed to never relive such moments.

So, indeed, if she'd had the slightest inkling that saving the lad would have the little calm she'd harnessed whistling away, she'd have fought the urge tooth and nail, with every fibre of her being.

She had enough worries already. Besides, he was the least obedient she'd met! He'd fought himself to his feet, defied her every instruction to rest,and accessed her entire home like it was his plaything!

Even now, he was busy sharpening at a knife, his skin aglow with sweat. She narrowed her eyes at him, thoroughly infuriated. Already, he looked as pallid as baking flour, his breath too slow and laboured to be normal.

He'd changed the towels she'd tied to the deep gash on his belly thrice already, and for a moment, she wondered if he understood what it meant to lose blood that much!

What an inconvenient, hard-nosed and reckless lad he was!

"You should get some sleep." He accessed the knife's blade under the streaks of light that broke through the wooden walls. "The dawn's breaking loose and you've barely caught a second of nap."

She stormed towards him, noting how his fingers were now starting to quiver. "Well, pardon me, if I'm not terrified that I'd sleep and wake to find a dead man next to me!"

He looked up at her. "If I'm the reason you're unable to catch some rest, I'll be obliged to leave. You have done a truckload of good for me already."

"You take a step out of here, and you'll be shot down, your blood pooling about my door." She glared at him. "Then, I'll be left to clean up the blood, dispose your body, and God help me, if I'm caught by some lousy mouthed folk, I'll be left to prove *nothing* to the Constables!"

He looked down at the knife in his hand. "I cannot be here for long. They'll kill you."

She matched to his front and knelt, so that she could stare at him, right in the eyes. "If the footsteps are of any worth to you, you'd know that those guys already found you." Her words burned with desperation. "I have lived here all my life. No one ever came here. Not even the drunkards…or the Constables. But in a night, I hear footsteps, not once, but twice!"

"If they were *them,* they'd have stormed in and had us killed." He gulped. "Perhaps, we've only worried too much."

She leaned closer to him, her anger ticking off like a bomb. "Don't take a step from here." Her voice was low with warning. "Whoever came around yesterday will be back. I'm sure of it. And they'll want to know where you went." She pointed a finger at him, the tip dangerously close to his eyes. "And my failure to provide them with details will get me killed!"

"So what?" He looked like he'd had enough of her. "Do I whisk you alongside me just because..."

"I am saying that you stay here till you get in

shape. Then, together we'll march to the Constables and file a report. I'll stand in as witness."

"And what does that change? How does that get you out of harm's way?"

She let down her hand. "Nothing may change, but at least, you'll be protected, in the Constable's custody."

"Those bloody Constables can give me no protection." He clenched his jaws. "They're weaker than rabbits drenched in rain."

She was going to make another statement when she noticed how red the new dressing around his wound had turned. The bleeding was getting out of hand.

Her head spun instantly in a three hundred and sixty degree, making her see red.

"I have had enough of your recklessness and preposterous attitude." She grabbed her reticule from the pole near the wall. "I'll go downtown, get some bandages, and some warm clothes. If I'm lucky, I'll get you pills and a healing balm." She slung the bag around her neck and shrugged on her coat, all in very quick moves.

"You stay here!" She shot him a hard warning. "And I hope for your sake that I'm not only rambling off. Do yourself some good, listen to me, and stay here."

"This is not any of your business." He tried to pull himself up but winced, pain and terror mingling in his gaze. "It's too dangerous," he croaked, voice cracking.

"Well, let me be the judge of that." She slipped her feet into her boots. "I swear I won't let them find you. Those good for nothing bastards." She let out a furious breath and then, looked at him, only to catch him already staring, a funny and unreadable expression on his face.

"What's that?" she muttered, unsure of whatever was going on in his head.

"What's what?"

She shrugged. "You're staring at me funny."

"See, I don't know, but you've got to promise me," he rasped, fear softening into desperation. "You don't seem like the kind to…listen." He clenched his jaws.

"You neither!" She began to storm towards him, but noticed his growing weakness and stopped halfway. "And that's why I have to go out there to find some means to keep you breathing! If only you'd listened to me and..."

"Promise me," he said, his voice a pitch higher

than hers, effectively stealing the words off her lips. "Promise me that you'll stay safe."

Mary met his eyes, every nerve alive with dread. "I swear." With that, she turned around and marched towards the trapdoor. Outside, she scanned the stretch of land in front of her, trying to catch a pair of wandering eyes or something that'd suggest a clandestine operation.

But then, just like she thought, no one lay in sight.

The gang never went anywhere in the day.

She looked back at the theatre one final time before running back to the street. *If she wasted any more time,* he'd die.

The street beyond was already stirring. A milk cart rattled past, its bells tinkling. A couple squares away, a pair of dockworkers cursed at each other over spilled sacks of coal. Mary tucked her coat tighter around herself. Mrs. Aldridge, one of her Ma's friends, had given her last winter, when she almost died of a frostbite.

She walked faster, too reminded of the strange lad in her home.

Mrs. Aldridge lived in the Strand, a part of Easter London that housed the business-inclined folks. She hadn't been to the Strand in months. The air there smelled of fresh paint and horsehair upholstery, not soot and seaweed, like Whitechapel.

Keeping her head low, she wound through narrow lanes, her legs moving quickly. At Mrs. Aldridge's door, Mary knocked twice—sharp, deliberate. The old seamstress opened almost immediately, as if she'd been waiting all morning.

"Mary," Mrs. Aldridge said, relief in her voice. Her shop was a riot of colour: bolts of silk and velvet stacked to the ceiling, spools of thread glittering like jewels. The scent of lavender sachets drifted in the air, soft and soothing.

"I need supplies," Mary said, her eyes perusing the corners in the shop. "Cloth, bandages, anything to help him heal."

"Who is *him?*" Mrs. Aldridge stared at her like she'd grown two sets of wings, her eyes impossibly narrowed.

Mary blinked. "Huh…I..."

"You better spill, Mary or you wouldn't find any help here."

Mary sighed, her shoulders falling alongside. She should have kept a tighter seal to her lips. "I found someone by the gutter." She avoided the woman's gaze, knowing how well she could read people's eyes. "He wasn't looking so well, so, I thought to care for him."

"Wasn't yesterday the day gunshots were heard at Whitechapel?"

"This matter is unrelated to the gunshots!"

"Listen, girl, I will not support this! Send him out of your home at once." She grabbed a box filled with silk. "These days, no one can be trusted."

"Can you just trust me this time, Mrs. Aldridge?" She met the woman's gaze, for the first time since she started explaining. "Please."

A shadow crossed Mrs. Aldridge's face, but she turned quickly and pulled a bolt of heavy wool from a shelf. "For warmth." She rummaged again and produced a length of fine silk—crimson, the same shade as that scrap Mary had pried from Will's hand.

"You'll need pockets," Mrs. Aldridge murmured, running her fingers over the fabric. "Slip these into the lining." She paused. "You're playing a dangerous game, child. I'd be evil to not let you know that."

Mary met her eyes. "I know."

With precise strokes, Mrs. Aldridge cut the silk and sewed it into the cloak's hem, her needle flashing silver. "I won't ask why. Just…be careful. The Crimson Fist grows bolder. They've taken two boys in the past week—no trace left."

THE MATCH GIRL

Mary's stomach twisted.

The seamstress handed over the finished cloak. Inside, hidden among folds, were three deep pockets. "For your things," she said softly. "And for his."

Mary slipped the cloak on, feeling the weight of Mrs. Aldridge's warning settle over her like a mantle. She pressed a small music box into the seamstress's hand—the one she'd rescued from the backstage clutter. "Payment."

Mrs. Aldridge smiled, a tired, gentle thing. "Does that still work?"

Mary shrugged. "You slam it on the head and it's as good as new." She chuckled, though shortly. "I hate to again be a bother, but do you have pills for pain? I'll need some healing balm too."

Mrs. Aldridge looked just ready to ask more words, but probably decided against it, a sigh the only sound escaping from her. "A minute, child." She vanished behind a door and returned, a small leather bag in her hand. "Everything is in there."

Mary beamed at her. "I owe you, Mrs. Aldridge." Barely had she finished uttering the words when she started running back home. For some reason, she felt good—good that she was doing the right thing, saving a person's life, fighting evil, all of that.

The journey home felt longer. Every footstep

echoed in her skull. She arrived only at midday, her limbs already tired from all the walking. She made haste to lift the trapdoor, hoping he wasn't dead yet.

Inside, the theatre was colder than she remembered. Dust motes floated in the shafts of light. Mary set down her satchel and called softly, "Will?"

Silence answered.

She climbed down, each rung creaking under her weight. On the blanket where he'd slept, she saw only an imprint—no sign of his bulk. Her throat went dry. She scanned the floor: the cloth bundle lay where she'd left it, untouched. But the spot where he'd lain was empty.

Every nerve in her lit up. Then she noticed it: a smear of dark crimson on the edge of the stairs—fresh. Mary knelt and touched it lightly. Warm. Not dried. Someone had bled here.

Her breath caught. She pressed her ear to the trapdoor hatch above. No sound but distant traffic and the drip of water from the roof. Then, faintly, a shuffle—just beyond the threshold.

She grabbed her knife, her cloak swirling around her, and inched toward the stain. Her heart hammered in her ears.

Had Will crawled out alone? Or had someone taken him?

A single match lay on the floor beside the blood, its tip burnt down to ash.

Her sanctuary had been violated.

And now, she had to choose: follow the trail into whatever darkness waited…or abandon the only home she'd ever known.

CHAPTER 5

She was gone.

And now, he had to be on the move. *The ledger*. He'd buried it behind the crates at Brine's Alley the night before they stabbed him and left him for dead. It was still out there. He laced his boots faster, too aware of the ticking clock. If the Crimson Fist had started sniffing around the theatre—if those footsteps they heard weren't just coincidence—then hiding in the theatre wasn't safety anymore.

It was bait.

He dragged on his coat and pressed a shaking hand to his side. The bandages Mary wrapped around the gash were now stiff with dried blood. He'd have to see a doctor soon. Otherwise, the wound would only get infected and increase his chances of dying.

Outside, the air was thick with fog and filth, curling around his face like a shroud. Every step felt like a rebellion against his body. But he knew he had to make it to Brine's Alley. That ledger held names. Dates. Money paid. Men sold. And probably, somewhere in its pages, his brother's fate.

The alley was darker than he remembered, crowded with crates and the stink of fish guts. He fell to his knees by the far wall, his fingers scrabbling against damp wood. Five minutes of relentless digging later, his hand struck something solid—an oilcloth.

He let out a relieved sigh. He'd found it—the one evidence he'd been stabbed for.

Mustering all of his strength, he yanked the bundle free, watching as sand tumbled off it. He patted the body and then, stood up to leave, only to hear the crunch of gravel behind him.

He turned, feeling the pain roar strongly through his skull. He noticed at once the men that stood afar off, their wristbands a sharp crimson. A quiet groan left his lips. How did they always find him?

Will clenched his jaws and astutely hid the ledger behind a crate, hoping in God's name that they didn't already catch sight of it. Heart in his throat, he staggered towards them, his hand pressing against the gash on his belly.

"What do you want?" His voice though weak and tired tumbled out with annoyance. "You're here to kill me again?"

They stared at him like they hadn't heard him talk.

"Why are you here..."

Before he could finish talking, a boot connected with his ribs, sending him tumbling against the crates, a strangled cry escaping his lips.

Oh, the pain.

"Well, look who wandered back from the grave," one of them sneered.

Two shadows loomed—one broad and sneering, the other wiry with a crooked jaw he remembered from the night they tried to finish him. The same night they'd laughed while he bled in the dirt.

Despite the pain that attacked his body, Will managed to forcea grin at them. "Looking for something, yes?"

One of them growled and drove a boot into his left shoulder. Will shut his eyes, feeling the fire lancedown his arm.

"Stupid little rat should've stayed dead," the

broader one muttered. "You and your bloody brother were always poking in places you didn't belong."

Will's breath hitched. They knew about Jonah. They really knew about him!

"May the bastard pay!"

However, before he could make any move, one of them kicked him again, right where the gash was. And like that, he was out, like light.

* * *

He came to with a tang of salt and cold mud in his nostrils. Whatever pain he'd felt before only felt little, in comparison to what now rocked his entire body. His eyelids only fluttered by an inch, allowing only little light into his soul. His hands and legs on the other hand felt as heavy as rocks. There was indeed no way he was making it out there by himself.

He clawed weakly at the dirt, annoyed.

The very death he'd tried to flee from was only by the corner, threatening to swallow him up whole.

"Please." He barely heard himself, but he knew he had to make some sound, to alert a passerby at least that he was there.

"Please." A hot tear slipped down his right cheek, but he didn't stop trying. He clawed even more at the sand, hating how the sun, out in full blast, heated up his already burning body, terrorizing him much more.

If there were any chance for survival meted out to him, he was sure it'd elapse in only few minutes. He closed his eyes, his lips already uttering a final prayer. *Someone would find the ledger and revenge on his behalf. They'd end the Crimson Fist and the reign of the other killers. They'd*—

His thoughts stilled, the sound of footsteps echoing in his head. They were light and hurried, reminding him all too much of the young lady he'd spent the night with.

With the last bit of strength in him, he pushed his eyes back open, only to see her running towards him, her dark hair riding with the wind, her cloak a bust of fire and light.

Mary.

Never had he thought he'd be happy to see her again.

She stumbled into the alley, breath ragged, face white. Her cloak billowed behind her, one hand holding up her skirts, the other gripping the tiny knife he'd seen with ear earlier in the day, before she left.

"Will," she whispered, her eyes wide with horror as she dropped to her knees beside him. "What have you done?"

He wanted to laugh but his ribs wouldn't let him.

"Had to get it," he murmured, catching solace in the shadow her body cast over his face.

"Had to get what?" She sounded like she'd cry, her voice a trembling mess.

"The ledger." He gulped, feeling the energy slip away from him slowly.

"What are you talking about? I see no ledger here!"

He closed his eyes. "I hid it. It's behind the crate just inches away from me."

"I don't care about no ledger!" Her hands ran all over his body, soft gasps erupting from her throat as she accessed his wounds. "All you were told was to stay indoors, in the theatre!"

"The ledger, please!" He couldn't help but feel a bit anxious. He'd been out, for only God knew how long. Perhaps, someone had come around and left with it. He couldn't be sure.

"Fine!" She rose to her feet, grumbling all the way down.

He heard her lift the crate.

"Is it there still?"

She marched down to him, the oilcloth in her hand. "You mean you risked your life because of this shrewd looking item?" She looked at it, unwrapping it just enough to see the ledger's worn, blood-smeared cover. Then her gaze flicked back to him, softer now. Fiercer.

"You idiot," she breathed. "You beautiful, bleeding idiot."

An unfamiliar emotion budded in his chest, but he chose to not pay attention to it. The ledger was safe with him and that was all that mattered.

Her hands moved fast—checking the worst of his injuries, propping him up, half-dragging, half-carrying him back through the fog-soaked streets. He didn't remember most of the journey. Only the sound of her voice, low and urgent in his ear, and the faint warmth of her hand pressed to his chest.

By the time they reached the theatre, he was barely conscious. She laid him down beside the dwindling fire and tossed the ledger aside.

"Now, you just keep talking to me." She hurried about the room, the sound of clanking bowls filling the air. "I need to know I'm not trying to save a dead man!"

He shut his eyes. "Tired."

"Well, you have to find a way to beat that down!" She arrived at his side and began to clean him up with a damp towel. "Your stubbornness should be able to keep a little drowsiness off the way, I believe."

"Too much was at stake. I couldn't stay back."

Her anger heated up the room, and he felt it, to his core. "Of course, you couldn't." She checked the gash on his belly and let out a hiss. "I just cannot understand you or your choices!"

"How did you find me?" He heard the sound of a zipper being drawn back. "Did you follow me?"

She let out a mirthless chuckle. "You wish." She poured a cool stinging liquid across the gash and then, used her mouth to blow on it. His body tingled in response, her hot breath sending a shot of adrenaline through him.

"Talk to me," he groaned, more out of the tension her soft feathery touches were building at the base of his belly.

"I followed the smear of blood on the stairs all the way to the docks." She began to rub an ointment all around the wound, her touch light, yet firm, igniting small patches of fire in every place her hands touched. "For the first time, I'm grateful for your bleeding. It made me find you."

She wrapped the wound with a clean roll of bandage, her moves all too practiced.

"Why do you care at all?" He struggled to open his eyes, desperate to catch whatever unsaid emotion lingered there.

She looked at him and shrugged. "I'd hate to see a man die when I could have helped." She moved away from him and changed the water in the bowl. "Did those bastards find you?" She glanced at him over her shoulders. "Did they do that to you?"

"Is this what you do when you find an injured Harry on the street? You pick them up and bring them home?"

Her eyes steeled, her emotions shielded and hidden from view. "You've got a very sharp tongue, I must say."

She put down the bowl of water and walked towards me. "You think you can sit? I've got some pain-killing pills for you."

"You won't answer my questions."

She let out a loud exhale. "You want your questions answered or your wounds healed?"

"Both." He watched as she tucked a curl of her hair behind her ear, his fingers aching to do the same to the other curl by the left.

She grabbed a canister from the bag containing

the supplies and poured out some pills into her palm. "Here. Your meds. You have to sit up so that you can swallow them with water."

He looked away from her. "I hate pills."

"Well, you've got to develop a liking towards them now." She propped closer and lifted his head gently from the pillow of rags. "Open your mouth now, will you?"

He tried to get her hand from around him, but his muscles could barely move an inch without failing. "You should stop," he groaned. "I can fight through the pain."

"Do as I say! Otherwise, I'll force these down your throat!"

He obliged, only after a couple more hot threats from her. Afterwards, he lay back on the pillow, his eyes shooting her a tight glare.

"What a good boy you are." She patted his arm and went about her duties, humming like she'd just won a lottery.

All was quiet for a long while, until she spoke again, her voice tinged with curiosity. "Tell me about the ledger." She stopped whatever she was doing and picked up the book, her hands running across the spine.

"What do you want to know?"

She settled next to him. "Everything there is to know. Why you'd risk your life for a mere book, why..."

"It's not just a mere book." He looked away, feeling the anger rise again. "It's more…a bunch of secrets the gang's willing to kill for."He exhaled, willing the pain to recede. "Names," he whispered. "Men…sold off by the gang, men that suddenly disappeared…records of their vile deeds."

He looked back at her, noting how closely she was watching him, a contrite look in her eyes. For a minute, he wanted to tell her everything, to trust her with the details…

After all, she'd saved his life.

And like she sensed his hesitation, she nodded encouragingly at him. "You can talk to me."

"My brother's name is in there."

The curiosity in her eyes vanished almost instantly, being replaced however with a hot desperation, almost like his brother was related to her too…like she could feel the exact pain he felt.

"I need to see what's in here," she said, her voice trembling.

He nodded, barely able to move. "His name is Jonah.Check the first two pages. You'll know what happened to him."

She opened the book, flipping through pages filled with scrawled names, dates, amounts. Then—

Her face drained of color. She turned the book toward him and jabbed her finger at a name inked in rust-colored blotches.

Jonah Hartley. Listed. Bought. Missing.

Mary closed the book with shaking fingers. "They're selling them," she whispered. "Men. Boys. Dock workers. Like meat."

Will felt the edges of the world curling again. "They'll come for me. For this."

Her breath hitched. "How long have you had this?"

"Long enough to have been dead decades ago."

She tied off the last bandage and sat back, her gaze flicking between him and the door. For a heartbeat, they simply stared—their shared fear heavier than any wound.

He reached out, brushing his fingers against hers. "I'm sorry I dragged you into this."

Her eyes glistened. She leaned forward—

A soft slip of paper on wood stopped them cold.

Mary's head snapped toward the trapdoor. A single note fluttered down, landing beside Will's boot. She snatched it up, her eyes scanning the jagged handwriting.

"Let me see."

She brought it to him, the fear clear in her eyes.

YOU SHOULD HAVE STAYED DEAD.

The candle sputtered as if in alarm. The pain he felt, though strong, couldn't have stopped him. He sat up at once, reading the line again and again.

"They're onto us," she whispered.

He swallowed, every nerve alive with dread. "Yes, and now, I have to run…or fight."

CHAPTER 6

No matter how hard she tried, she just couldn't push the contents of the letter aside. The gang had surely found him. They'd been responsible for the footsteps she'd heard on the two different occasions, it was not a random drunk man that lost his way, but a member of the deadliest gang in Whitechapel.

And they sure knew she was harbouring him.

Oh goodness.

What exactly had she brought herself into?

She willed herself to remain calm before facing Will, trying to make sense of whatever he was doing. Ever since he'd received the note, he'd been doing different things—sharpening blades, pacing about, muttering different words, running through the ledger, writing things on the wall, and a couple other things that pushed her to frenzy.

"Can you..." She gulped. "Can you please stop and listen to me?"

He began to lace his boots. "I am sorry I had to bring you into this."

Panic bit at her throat. "Where are you going?"

"Somewhere they won't find me, anywhere."

"I'm sorry?"

He looked up at her, his gaze hardening. "Is there an issue?"

She lost whatever sanity she had left. "You want to leave? Just like that?" Incredulousness poured out with her words. "You think you're the only one in danger now? I risked everything to keep you hale... and hearty. And now that you've got what you want, you just want to pull out of the game?"

"We have had this conversation before."

"And I'm repeating it because the previous one yielded no fruit!" She could feel her hands begin to tremble, and she so much hated it. What guts he had, to put her in such tight spot!

"Once I'm out of here, they won't bother you."

"You speak like a soothsayer with prophetic skills!"

He grabbed the ledger from across the stool in

the middle of the room. "Listen, I'm grateful to you. Sincerely. But I have nothing else to offer you. I cannot possibly stay here any longer or tell you to jump the streets with me."

The latter option sounded too good to her ears, and she wondered for the briefest second if she was crazy in the head.

"Well, you have to do something but leave!" She glared at him. "I've survived winters, fires, street patrols, everything—and no one ever found me! But you… you show up half-dead and now death's knocking on the door!"

She didn't mean it—not really. But the panic rose in her throat like bile, tasting of dread and betrayal. Her voice cracked. "You brought them here. You..."

Will staggered forward, towards her, his face drawn and pale. "I didn't ask you to save me."

Those words punched the breath from her. She saw the flicker of pain cross his face before he turned away.

Then, silence swelled, thick and sharp.

She eyes his back, her gaze tracing the trees of purple-black bruises…and the reopened wound darkening the cloth at his ribs. He was in pain…a lot of it. And her words were only making the matters worse.

His body trembled slightly, teeth clenched from holding back pain.

Her anger softened. Just a little.

"I didn't mean any of what I said," she said quietly, remorseful. "I just—this was the only place that was *mine*." Her voice faltered. "And now it's gone."

Will nodded, grim. "I don't have too many options. I wish I could keep you safe."

"Then, let me come with you." She refused to consider her words much. Refused to accept her maddening thoughts. "I'll tend to your wounds and see to it that you're fine."

He turned around to look at her, his gaze tearing through her, to her very soul. He took a step forward, his eyes never leaving, never wandering.

She gulped. "Please."

"Why?" He took another step forward. "You want to throw your life and home away for a man you only just met? No one I've met is ever that crazy."

"I told you before. I read people."

He kept moving closer, a step at a time. "And when you read me, what do you see?"

His face was now closer, the electric blue in his eyes sending her heart racing. "It's not about what I see." She dared to take a step toward him, her gaze swallowing up hiswhole. "It's what I hear."

They only stopped moving when they were inches away, the letter long forgotten, the only sounds in their ears that of their wildly thumping hearts.

"What is it that you hear?"

She shot him a small smile. "I'll tell you if you let me leave with you."

To her blatant surprise, he didn't press the matter any further. He just looked away, a small sigh escaping his lips. "I cannot promise you of a luminescent future…and I certainly cannot change this concrete mind of yours."

Not like the presentcontained anything of interest she could hold on to. Other than the matchsticks she sold, her daily routine wasn't worth a farthing.

"Let's plan how we get back at those bastards." She felt the fear lift off her shoulders for a second. "We have the ledger. We'll take it to the Constables and..."

"We cannot do that." He motioned for her to come closer. "See…some pages are missing…the pages that contain their transactions, signatures, and blood prints. Before the Constables, this is just a mere fabrication that has no ground."

She studied the page numbering closely, and indeed, certain pages were missing. "Why then did you protect this with your life, if…" She looked at him, wide-eyed. "If it's of no worth?"

He shook his head. "It is…only in the presence of the other half." He shut the ledger and began to wrap it with the oilcloth again. We have to get the other half from them."

"How exactly are we going to get that done?"

"Just how I got this from them."

She placed her hand on his arm lightly, stopping him from making any more moves. "Care to acquaint me with that?"

"I snuck into the office while working on their fields."

"Did you stop to consider that you no longer work for them? They know your face. You cannot sneak in without getting noticed."

He stilled, realization dawning on him.

"But then, I have an idea."

* * *

THEY MET Tommy behind a bakery that stank of coal and yeast. He was thin as a shadow and sharp as a crow, with a cap too big for his head and fingers that never stayed still.Mary had met him on the streets one night, and they'd had a long talk, the focus of their conversation fixed on anything and everything.

The good old days…

He was a good lad—a poor orphan like she was, with eyes thatalways seemed to catch everything.

And for that very reason did she—they—now need his help.

"Mary!" Heran down to the side of the fields where she and Will stood. "Didn't expect to see you here, but I'm glad of it!" His smile grew. "So, tell me, *pumpkin*, what brings you around these parts?" He glanced briefly at Will. "And why, tell me, is he staring at me with so much loathe? Is he perhapsyour betrothed?"

"Tommy!" she cautioned, feeling the heat rise to her cheeks.

"Forgive me." He pressed his hands together in apology, but his eyes remained bright withmischief.

Mary sighed. Thank goodness she'd decided to let her hair down. Otherwise, her deep red cheeks would have been quite a sight for all.

A betrothed?

She almost laughed. That would be top-class luxury, even for someone like her.

"Either way, you owe me," Tommy said, jabbing a finger into herarm. "Last time I warned you about a copper sweeping the row? That saved your skin. You know it."

Mary crossed her arms. "And I gave you two meat pies for it."

Tommy sniffed. "Not enough."

Will leaned forward, bruised but taller than Tommy by nearly a head. "We're not asking for a bedtime story…or friendly banter." He shot poor Tommy a hard look."We need drop points. Routes. She says you're good at that." Will eyed him warily, like he couldn't believe him to be any useful to his plans. "We want anything you've seen the Crimson Fist doing near the docks."

Tommy looked at Will. "You the lad they're looking for?"

Will tensed.

Tommy grinned. "Thought so."

Mary pulled a coin from her boot. She was fast running out of pennies to spare, and she really hoped Will got a stash somewhere! Otherwise, they'd both starve to death by the morrow.

"Tell us where they stash their tributes and we'll owe you two pies."

Tommy took the coin from her and bit it. "Three pies. And a knife."

Mary sighed. "Fine. But it better be good."

Tommy beamed at her. "We have a deal. I'll meet you behind the old textile mill when the sun is down."

"Thank you."

The walk to the mill was quiet, the atmosphere buzzing strangely with electricity. Mary tried to catch his gaze, but he just looked straight ahead, like a soldier on a war mission.

"You have some pennies to spare?" She waited for him to look at her, but he didn't, not for a minute. "I am only a tad close to being penniless."

"I have a gold coin."

Her eyes almost popped out of their sockets. A gold coin was equal to about fifty pennies—more than enough money for a proper meal. "Indeed?"

He kept quiet, reminding her again of his sour mood. She frowned. He didn't talk a lot, sure enough, but at least, he did talk more often than he was doing now.

A couple minutes later, they arrived at the crumbling brick wall behind the old textile mill. They sat together on the high ground, their legs folded beneath them.

Mary set her bag on her lap. She'd stuffed in a few supplies, his pills, some wads of clean bandages, and a tin of bread. "We should change your bandages."

He looked away, his jaw still tight. "No."

She frowned. Whatever had gotten him so grumpy? "Why would you say no? You clearly don't look good."

He clenched his jaws and shut his eyes, his breathing the only sound from him. "Are you betrothed to any man?"

She blinked, completely thrown off by his question. *What did it matter to him if she was betrothed?* She watched him breathe, a thousand questions spinning around her mind. *Was he disturbed, perhaps by the fact that she probably belonged to some man?* Before she could regain her composure, he looked back at her, his eyes soft, but not revealing anything beyond the surface.

Oh, darn him!

"Mary?"

A shiver danced down her spine. For the first time, he was calling her name, his voice trembling with desperation and need and—

"It's my last!"

She and Will immediately looked away, towards the direction the sound came from. Below, a boy—no older than Will—stood surrounded by gang men. He was shouting, refusing to hand over a coin.

A blow silenced him.

Mary gasped, her hand flying to her mouth.

He hit the ground hard, coughing blood.

Will moved before Mary could stop him, fury twisting his features.

Terrified, she grabbed his armtight, stopping him in time. "No! You'll only get him—and yourself—killed."

Will froze. His fist trembled. The men kicked the boy once more, then walked off laughing.

Will swallowed hard. "Just how many of them are out there?"

"Too many," Mary whispered, fighting for words that'd keep him calm. "That's why we need to be smarter. We get in, we get out. No heroics."

He didn't answer.

He just sat back down, a pained look to his face. Mary settled next to him, and then, lit a single stub of candle. Then, together, they poured over the notes Will had made in the past—drawings of crates, marked corners, times, and names. They were close to something, they could feel it.

They just didn't know what yet.

The candle was burning low when Tommy reappeared, breathless, and pale under the grime. "They're coming," he rasped. "And they've got your name."

He looked at Will. "And hers too."

CHAPTER 7

"Tommy, tell me what happened," Mary quipped, the words pouring off her lips one by one.

Will watched as Mary paced about in circles, her fists tightly rounded about the roots of her hair. She sure was anxious, and unready for the kind of life he lived...or rather had chosen to live, the moment he discovered that the gang was involved in his brother's sudden disappearance.

It was a fight *he* had to take on, and so, he truly didn't understand why she was choosing to take the risk with him. Or why she was so willing to throw everything away, without even properly getting to know him. Or how he had it in him, at such perilous times to be struck by her beauty.

He'd caught himself staring at her one too many times, the small shy smile on his face lighted by his intrigue for her wittiness and stubbornness. She always had a plan…always knew what to do, and he adored even more how she quietly supported him, not pressing until he spoke.

Her touches, tender and light, had soothed the pain, and he couldn't even piece together the mechanisms of such! He loved when she stared at him, her big black eyes shining with such radiance and—

"What's wrong with him?"

Mary caught his gaze at that moment, a small frown tugging at her eyebrows. "Will?"

He gulped, fast losing grip of his reins. She had never once called him by name. All along, he'd just been a lad in need of help and care. But now…things were quickly changing.

"He's staring at you like that while trouble looms ahead and you say you two aren't betrothed to each other?"

Tommy's words instantly pulled him out of his trance. The boy was too much of a chatterbox, never helping himself to some caution.

"I was thinking of something." He glared at Tommy. "Go on with whatever you were saying."

Mary walked up to him, her hand resting against his forehead. "He's got a fever. I fear he is..."

"I'm fine," he muttered, pushing her hand away. There was no way he could focus with her constantly touching him like that. He nodded at Tommy. "I don't think we've got plenty of time. Hurry and spill what you found."

The stormy look that had once filled Tommy's face returned. "I think the blokes from the gang are out there. They're looking for us."

Will's grip on the ledger tightened. "What do you mean, looking for us?"

Tommy's words tumbled out in a rush. "I was heading back to you, right? I took the long way, through the warehouses, just to be safe. But somethin' didn't feel right. The streets were too quiet—too still. Usually, there's some kind of noise, even at night. But there was nothing. Then I spotted 'em. Two men, walking together, looking like they knew exactly where they were going. One sure looked like one of 'em Constables."

"The gang have people in the Force." Will shook his head.

Mary's brow furrowed. "Did they see you?"

"No, no, I kept my distance. Stayed in the shadows." Tommy's hands shook as he ran them through his hair. "But they weren't just walkin' about. They stopped by the old depot and one of 'em pulled out a piece of paper. A bloody list, I think. I didn't get a clear look, but I saw what was written: The Hartley ledger." He looked at Will. "That's what they were after."

Will's pulse quickened, his voice tight. "The ledger?"

Tommy nodded, his face pale in the flickering light. "Yeah. They were searchin' for the same thing we are. Maybe even for us. They—one of 'em—a big bloke with a scar down his face, started looking around, real careful, like he was expectin' someone to pop out. That's when I realized. They're lookin' for you two. They're after the ledger. Something about a second piece."

Mary's eyes darted to the fields below where they stood, then back at Tommy. "How did you get away?"

Tommy's mouth was dry. "I didn't. Not easy. One of 'em started coming down the alley, real slow, so I hid behind the crates. Then, outta nowhere, another one popped up. I barely made it out without them hearing me. I don't know how they're tracking us, but I'm sure as hell not stickin' around to find out."

His eyes shifted nervously to the door, then back

at Will and Mary. "The worst part? I heard the sirens wailin'. The bloody constables are out there now—could be they've already spotted us. We gotta move, or we're done for."

Mary didn't hesitate. "We're not running." Her voice was firm. "The Constables only arrest the bad guys. We did nothing wrong!"

"Many of the Constables are meshed deep in the evil. The ledger has all the records of their names and evil deeds. If they're chasing us, it's because they don't want any of that out." Will shook his head in annoyance. "It's also why the gang is hard to eradicate. We've just got to fight back."

Tommy blinked at him. "You sure about that, mate? The whole bloody city's searchin' for you. I think hiding is the best bet now."

"I'm sure," Will replied. His voice was steady now, despite the fear simmering beneath. "We can't just disappear. They'll never stop hunting us. We take the fight to them."

Tommy swallowed hard, but then, a grin broke through the tension. "Well, now I'm glad I've got a front-row seat for this show."

The sirens grew louder.

"I need to run. I'll meet you later tonight at the

theatre." Tommy waved and vanished, just as smoothly as he'd appeared.

Will grabbed Mary's hand and together, they ran back to the theatre, not for a minute stopping. Mary kept muttering something about not running into any of the Constables, her fear solid. At first, he'd wanted to ask questions, but eventually decided against it, her troubled eyes enough warning for him.

The moment they arrived at the theatre, Mary secured the braces to the trap door, her breath bursting out in pants. "Thank goodness, thank goodness. It could have been horrible back there."

The theatre groaned as Will paced across the dust-smeared boards beneath the stage. Mary settled on a collapsed set piece, watching him with narrowed eyes and clenched hands. "Now, I see it. They won't stop," she said. "Not until we're dead or the ledger's gone."

Will stopped pacing. "We have to find the second piece, fast. They know that we have the first piece.If anything, that would propel them to get rid of any other piece that'd make what is with us intangible and useless."

Mary arched an eyebrow. "Then, we have to find a way in…not as workers, definitely." She rose to her feet. "Besides, I heard some blokes say the gang cleaned out their office a while back."

"Not the main office," Will said, his voice low and deliberate. "There was a place deeper in. A storeroom by the docks—one they used during the strike when the union men raided the main building."

She tilted her head. "And you're just remembering this now?"

"I didn't think it mattered. Not until…" He looked away, jaw tight. "Not until Tommy said they thought we had the other piece of the ledger."

Mary's expression softened just slightly. "So what's in this secret storeroom?"

"Crates of old logs, backups. Some of the bosses didn't trust the new clerks, so they kept double records. I ran errands there—saw where the keys were kept."

Mary stood slowly, brushing dust from her skirt. "If there's a chance it's there, we go tonight. Before word spreads any further."

Will nodded. "We'll need Tommy."

* * *

THE BOY ARRIVED JUST after nightfall, grinning despite the tension in his shoulders. He carried a sack half his size and a dagger strapped awkwardly to his belt.

"You two are getting good at being ghosts," he said, ducking through the hidden entrance. "But this one'll be tricky."

"Can you get us there unseen?" Mary asked.

Tommy gave a mock bow. "Through the sewers. Dirty, dark, and smells worse than a corpse pit, but it'll do."

Mary gave a curt nod. "Then let's go."

The descent into the underbelly of the East End was not for the faint-hearted. The air beneath the city was thick with rot and water, the sound of trickling filth echoing in narrow stone tunnels. Mary held a rag to her nose.

Will kept a steady hand on her back as they moved, intermittently checking on her to be sure she was fine.

"Remind me," she muttered, "why do all important secrets have to be hidden in places like this?"

"It's the Victorian way," Will said dryly. "Grime and guilt."

Tommy snorted ahead of them. "Oi! Less talk, more shuffle. We're near the sluice now."

They emerged behind the old depot on Bentwharf Lane just past midnight. The docks loomed in silhouette, half-lost in fog, but the warehouse itself was quiet. Abandoned but not forgotten.

Will crept forward, memory guiding his steps. The rusted padlock was still there, a broken crate leaned against the wall beside it.He reached behind It and pulled loose a stone.

Beneath it was a key, silvery and shiny.

Mary gave him a look. "You're full of surprises."

He didn't answer—just slipped the key into the lock and opened the door.

The room inside smelled of mildew, ink, and old paper. The walls were lined with shelving, though most of it had collapsed under the weight of time and moisture. Crates of rotting ledgers sat half-open, their contents furred with mould.

Will rifled through them, careful but quick. Mary joined him, holding the lantern high.

"There." Her fingers brushed something solid beneath a torn burlap sheet. She knelt and pulled out a thick, leather-bound book, the corners worn and water-stained.

Will's breath caught. He took it gently, opened to the first page—shipment lists, backdated entries, payment records.

He flipped through faster, his breath growing at similar rate.

Names. Numbers. Codes.

And then—

He froze.

Mary noticed. "What is it?"

He turned the page slowly. Page after page of dirty secrets. Payments. Codes. Names—dock men, merchants, constables. Then,a name, near the bottom.

Jonah Hartley.

His brother's name. Scrawled in the same looping hand I'd seen on shipment lists. Crossed out in red ink. The ink had bled through the page, angry and permanent.

"They erased him," he whispered.

Mary looked up sharply. "What?"

"They didn't just kill him. They made sure no one would ever know he'd been there."

Will's throat closed. "They had him on the books. As if he were stock. And then they'd just... erased him."

Mary was silent for a beat. Then she crouched beside him, her hand covering his. "We'll make them bastards pay."

He looked at her, eyes shadowed. "He was just trying to live." His voice caught somewhere deep in his throat. "Just trying to live."

Mary was going to take his hand in hers when footsteps sounded above. Loud. Fast.

Tommy burst into the doorway, chest heaving. "Will. Mary. We've got to go."

"What?" Mary asked, rushing to her feet.

"They followed me. I didn't know—I didn't see them, I swear it. I thought I lost 'em at the canal, but..." he broke off as a shrill wail cut through the air.

Sirens.

Will grabbed the ledger. "Out the back—now!"

Tommy led them through a narrow hallway, the fire escape rusted but intact. Shouts echoed from the main corridor. A light flared through the slats in the door they'd just left behind.

Mary didn't look back as they ran into the dark. "Darn these Constables!" She screamed. "We did nothing wrong and yet, they chase us like we are the gang they ought to be after."

But the sound of that siren followed them, louder than any gunshot.

Will ran faster.

They sure were ruined.

CHAPTER 8

Oh goodness! If only Tommy had stayed with them! Mary sliced the lad's back with a glare, but he was too busy fleeing for life to notice.

Shouts rang out—deeper, rougher. This time, it didn't sound like the Constables. Mary's eyes flicked to the side as shadows spilled in through the gaps between the crates. Gang members. Dozens of them. Some with knives drawn, others with clubs and crowbars. One pointed straight at Will, his face squeezed like he had tasted gall.

"There! That's the boy! Get the book!"

Mary's heart thudded against her ribs. Thee ones were surely not giving any grounds for negotiation. Once they were caught, they'd immediately be killed and stashed with the regular trash.

THE MATCH GIRL

A voice called out, "Surround 'em!"

They ducked behind crates, but they were boxed in.

"What do we do?" Tommy shrieked, horrified.

Mary's gaze shot to the floor—an old oil drum had leaked across the planks, a sticky sheen glowing faintly in the dim light. Her fingers closed around the matchbox in her pocket.

Will caught her eye. "Mary, don't!"

"They won't stop chasing us, Will." Her fingers trembled as she struck the match. "That happens, and we'll be out cold by morning."

A flame. A decision.

She tossed it into the oil.

A roar swallowed the warehouse. Flames ignited the floorboards, then leapt upward, catching the beams, racing toward the roof like a creature unleashed.

Screams. Footsteps. Panic.

"Move!" Tommy shouted, tugging Will. "Tunnel now!"

They ran, half-blinded, choking. Will stumbled but kept going, arm slung over Tommy's shoulder. Mary stayed at his side, shielding the ledgers inside her coat.

They pushed into the narrow tunnel, the one

they'd come through, and flames licked at their heels, smoke coiling through the dark.

Somehow, they made it out. Coughing, bruised, hearts hammering.

"Thank goodness!" Tommy breathed out the soot that had powdered his nostrils. "I was certain I'd die there."

"You should have been more careful!" Mary screamed, her eyes following the fire. For some reasons that shook her to her core, it wasn't just burning down the warehouse. It was spreading too quickly, across farms, barns, houses, and—

She stopped looking, the panickedscreams of the town piercing her heart like arrows. She'd done that. She'd started the fire. Now, they'd have nowhere to sleep.

"Are you okay?"

Her gaze flew back to Will. He was bent over, his skin sweaty and crushed with pain. "Will!" She ran to him and knelt before him so that their gazes could meet. "Did you get yourself injured?"

"It's nothing," he ground out, his words a quiet hiss. "We have to leave now. A fire won't stop the gang."

She tried to access his wounds and bandages, but he stopped her in time, his gaze commanding her to action. Anger, thick and stubborn, budded within her but she rose to her feet nevertheless. He was in so much pain, and yet, he wouldn't let her help, or even let her into his head.

"Fine! If you won't let go of your haughtiness and let me offer some help, I'll with every ecstasy in me leave you be!"

"Are we leaving for the theatre?" Tommy cut in, looking bored already. "If the fire won't stop those folks, then we better keep moving."

Will fought to stand straight, his gaze fixed on something ahead. "We have to run. The fire's traveling fast, and I fear it already burned down the theatre." He glanced briefly at her, his eyes burning with anger, regret and pain.

Mary was going to shoot him a glare equally as hot when his words dawned on her. *Her theatre could become non-existent only in minutes!* Her eyes grew big, the adrenaline fast pumping into her legs.

"Not my theatre!"

She sped down the roadway, the sting of the wind sharp against her face. She had too many of her personal items in that building—her clothes, her ma's keepsakes, the cloaks Mrs. Aldridge sew her, her knives, the—

She slowed to a stop just minutes later, watching as smoke curled around the rooftop.

"No," Mary breathed. Her body quivered, and for the space of two breaths, she could hardly process a thought.

Will and Tommy arrived a second later, their raging breaths thundering in her ears.

"I didn't want this."

Will's voice kicked her out of her daydream. She let out a sound of trepidation and then, kicked forward, not thinking or caring about the tongues of fire licking up everything.

Soot streaked her face as she ran for the back entrance. The fire had spread. Sparks had jumped—maybe from the warehouse, maybe from some cruel trick of fate.

Her safe haven was burning.And that was all she could think of.

"Mary!" She'd never heard Will sound that perturbed. He'd always sounded like he was the Governor of some Constituency; in control, cool and composed.

"Don't go back! I beg your pardon!"

But she didn't listen.

She disappeared through the narrow door, vanishing into the smoke. The flame bloomed bright in the dark, and for a second, it lit every corner of the room—the threadbare bedding, the old theatre drapery, the drawings on the wall she'd made when she was smaller and dreaming.

Seconds passed—longer. Then longer still.

The music box! Her music box!

She sighed in relief on catching sight of the cabinets. It was the one thing the fire hadn't touched. She drew through the compartments, coughing and choking on the smoke. She found the box a second later and cradled it against her chest.

She was going to search for some other item to salvage when someone suddenly grabbed her from behind.

"You promised me that you'll stay safe!"

Will's thunder rushed to her, totally raw, raucous and unexpected. She blinked against the smoke, noting how his face was torn both with relief and anger.

Her mind began to think in one too many strange directions. Had he indeed been so bothered to come along looking for her? She almost smiled. At least, not with the next words that tumbled out of his mouth—the very reminder of the reality she was fast losing grip of.

"You almost had yourself killed!"

"I never promised that I'd stay safe—"

Her words died somewhere in her throat the moment he lifted her off her feet and threw her across his shoulders. The world tumbled upside down before her eyes, the fire chasing ardently after Will's feet.

He was just going to make the last step out when something exploded in the distance and sent them both flying, out of the wreckage to the muddy fields outside.

Will landed first, his body bearing all the weight of her fall, the music box the only thing between them. Eyes wide as saucers, she stared down at his face, breathing in the hot air he exhaled, their thrumming heartbeats pounding in unison.

For the faintest second, she became oblivious to the cacophony that filled the air. Her body, lit up by the strangest and most pleasurable of fires, hummed and hummed, welling up in her a desire to just remain there, in his arms.

His face was impossibly beautiful.

Awe-struck, a self-willed finger of hers hovered across his face, the pad of it drawing lines across the soot powdering his skin.

"I'm pleased to see that you're not incapacitated, like I am." His eyelids flashed open, scaring the daylight out of her. *What had come over her?* In a shrug of his arm, she was off him, his wrecked self staggering to its feet. He closed his eyes for a second, his pale face torn with pain.

"A music box, Mary? You risk your life for that?"

She looked weakly at Tommy, her shoulders heaving, from a fusion of exertion and the fiery contact she'd just had with that handsome bloke! "It was all I could carry."

Behind her, the building groaned. Flames roared louder as a section of the roof caved in. Sparks billowed skyward. The theatre—their shelter, their secret—was no more.

"You try that sort of thing again, and I won't hesitate to chain you somewhere!"

Her vivacious side roared to life, stirred up by the fire in his voice. "Well, pardon me for wanting to save a little for my poor self." She didn't desire to scream, but for some reasons she was sure was tied to the frustration she felt, she did.

How was she liking the poor injured lad so fast?

"He just saved your life!"

She silenced Tommy with a glare. "You know nothing about anything!"

"I warned you not to start that fire."

Her gaze was fast back on Will. "So, it's my fault

now? You will blame me for doing the one ingenious thing that saved our lives?"

He opened his mouth to say something, but decided against it. "I owe you," he later said, gulping. "I apologize for the loss of your home. I promise I'll compensate you in some way."

His words killed the fire inside of her. She looked away from him, unsure of what to do…or say. "They were bound to found the theatre anyway." She looked further away from them. "We ruined their warehouse. They'd want revenge too. So, either way, the theatre would be burned down."

Tommy's voice cut through the smoke-thick air. "You sure about this? This place… it's yours."

"It was mine," Mary whispered, turning around on her feet. "Let's go."

Out the back, they walked quietly past the rusted ladders and into the alley, feet pounding the cobblestones slick with soot. The fire roared behind them now, louder than the sirens.

Tommy led the way, ducking behind barrels and empty market stalls as they wound around the lanes. Mary on the other hand would not stop stealing glances at Will, her mind trying hard to process reasons for her deep infatuation.

He was only a stranger she'd met a couple of days

ago. So why? What had made her go that crazy in the head?

He didn't even seem to have the slightest bit of adoration for her. Even now, he was smoothly avoiding her, walking faster and keeping a scowl on his face like he did whenever he didn't want to talk.

She let out a tired sigh.

His wounds had begun to bleed again, and she desired even more strongly to tie him somewhere with heavy duty chains and then, see to it that he recuperated.

He was too stubborn, digging relentlessly until he found some treasure. And in as much as it irritated her at the moment, she couldn't help but be drawn by him. His stubborn gaze. His unyielding determination. His squared shoulders. His working jaws. His burly arms. Everything.

She liked him enough to not even be bothered much that she'd lost her home. She had nothing. Yet, in his arms some minutes ago, she'd felt safe and secure, like she had it all.

If only she understood what rare madness had befallen her.

"I have to find somewhere to read this." He patted the sack under his coat. "We can't lose it now."

"We've got to expose the evil in there," Mary said. "To someone who'll listen."

Will's face hardened.

"There's a name here. A constable—paid weekly, high sum. If he's working for them, maybe someone else in the force isn't."

Tommy gave a grin, but it was crooked, wary. "That's a dangerous hope, Mary."

"And the only one we've got," she said.

A pounding noise cut through the moment. Boots on stone. Close. Too close. Will stuffed the ledger back in the sack. "Out the side—now."

They burst into the alley behind the shed, slipping like rats through the cracks of a waking city.

"There's nowhere to go," Tommy wailed.

"There is one more place."

Will looked at her. "Where?"

She stared of in the distance. "Father O'Malley."

* * *

Mary didn't say a word until they were at Father O'Malley's. Will sure looked like he had questions to ask, but his weak and bleeding body only made her see red. She pounded on Father O'Malley's iron door untilit creaked open.

Father O'Malley stood there in his plain cassock, silver hair tousled, lantern in hand. He blinked at the smoke on their clothes, the bruises, the scorch marks.

"Well." His voice was rough with sleep. "You three look like you've walked straight out of hell."

Mary didn't argue. She looked up at him, eyes rimmed with ash and stubbornness. "We have nowhere else to go."

The priest's gaze dropped to the bundle in her arms—the music box and the satchel dangling from her neck. Then to Will, leaning heavily against Tommy, pale and bleeding again.

Father O'Malley hesitated.

He had rules. Lines not to cross. Trouble not to welcome.

But then he saw the look in Mary's eyes—rage and grief twisted together, the look of someone who had lost everything but refused to be broken.

He stepped back, jaws clenched, his eyes scouring the dark for wandering eyes. "Inside. Quickly."

The door shut behind them with a thud that echoed in the old church walls. Candles flickered in the corner near the altar. Dust caught the light like smoke. The stone beneath their feet was cold.

"Lay him on the front pew," the priest said,

already fetching a pitcher of water and linen from the back. "I'll see to the bleeding."

Tommy helped Will down. Will grunted in pain but said nothing, clutching the ledger close to his side.

Mary hovered, the music box still pressed to her chest.

Father O'Malley returned with a quiet sigh and knelt beside Will, cleaning the gash along his shoulder. "The city's burning tonight," he muttered. "You had a hand in that?"

Mary didn't speak. Neither did Will.

The priest glanced up. "I'll take that as a yes."

He rose slowly, wiping his hands. "You can stay the night. But if soldiers come, or the gang, or anyone else—this church is sanctuary. I won't see blood spilled on this floor."

Mary nodded. "We'll be gone by dawn."

She had no idea whatever it was she was uttering.

But Father O'Malley looked at her—really looked—and then gave a low, tired sigh. "Stay as long as you need. Just don't bring the fire with you."

Will was already drifting into sleep, his head resting on Tommy's folded coat.

Mary sat a few paces away, knees pulled up, the firelight from a distant candle dancing across her face. She really wanted to help the lad. She hated the frown that sat permanently between his brows. He rarely smiled, rarely allowed himself a moment of rest, even when his body was clearly in need of it.

She opened the ledger on her lap.

Pages of names. Payments. Codes and marks.

And there—crossed out in red—Jonah Hartley.

She traced the name with one finger, her jaw tightening. That one line explained everything. Why they'd hunted Will. Why the gang was willing to kill to silence him.

Mary's eyes flicked to Will. His breathing was slow, even.

She had to do something. Anything.

Mary setthe music box on the pew beside her. It was blackened and blistered, but it still played. Still sang of the life she once dreamed of.

A life stolen. A brother buried. A city steeped in secrets.

And the fire had only just begun.

CHAPTER 9

Her hair, dark and shiny as a coin, was packed into a chignon, her eyes oiled with a sheen more beautiful than the midnight sky. Sheheld his hands, a radiant smile parting her lips ever so slightly, her legs moving in step with his as they waltzed to a song hummed by her music box.

He pressed his cheek to her hair, breathing her in. She smelled of lavender and ash and the faintest trace of matchsticks. Time slowed, the rhythm between them growing into something so sacred he wished he could store in a box.

No one watching. No one chasing. Just two souls, worn by the world, suspended in peace.

"I could stay like this forever," Will whispered into her hair.

Mary tilted her face up to his. "Then do."

He leaned in, just enough to brush his lips over her forehead, soft as breath.

His eyes fluttered open, slowly, like he was afraid he'd lose grip on such perfect moment. He could still feel the zap of electricity at the base of his belly, the chills travelling down his spine, thesoftness of her curls…

A cold gust of air swept across his bare feet, plucking him out too quickly from the warm dream. Jaws clenched, he pulled himself up from the wooden pew, the faint smell of smoke in the air reminding him of the previous night.

The ledger!

Panic-stricken, he looked about him, only to find the leather-bound ledger open on his knee while Mary slept beside him, her head resting on the music box. The silvery light that poured in through the church's windows had made home on her forehead, making her look almost irresistible. She was the prettiest damsel he'd ever seen.

He looked away almost immediately, feeling the weight of the ledger tear at his leg. A lot had to be done. He'd worry about his heart afterwards.

He looked around, hoping to catch sight of someone. The church was still… too still.

He closed the ledger and rubbed his eyes. Every name inside felt like a weight in his gut.Besides, the more he held on to the book, the more the people he dragged into his duel with the Crimson Fist, Mary, Tommy, and now, the Priest.

He glanced toward the sacristy door, half-expecting Father O'Malley to appear with hot tea and a scolding. He'd caught the man's wary gaze the other night, and he knew well enough that they'd be met with some Scripture readings on the right way to live.

Will smiled, the smile faltering only when he caught movement by the side. He turned his head in time to catch a tall man slipping through the priest's door, the dim light revealing a serpent tattoo coiling around his knuckles.

Will stood, heart stuttering in his chest. He crept forward, pressing himself against a cold pillar. From there he could just make out the murmur of voices.

"You're late." Father O'Malley didn't flinch. He just looked on, the softness in his posture gone.

The man stepped closer, his face grim beneath his hood. "Couldn't move sooner. They've tightened the watch at the docks. Someone tipped them off. They're scared."

"Good," the priest said flatly. "Let them be."

The tattooed man folded his arms. "You have it?"

O'Malley nodded slowly and drew a page from inside his coat. Will took a step closer, curious. The sheet was brittle and aged. The priest held it up to the candlelight, studying the writing scribbled in ink.

"Mary and Will risked everything to retrieve this," he said, more to himself than the man before him. "But if the wrong eyes ever see it…"

Will stilled. *What were they talking about?*

O'Malley brought the flame to the edge of the paper.

The man shifted. "Are you sure?"

"No one else dies for this," the priest murmured. "Not the orphans. Not the innocent. And not them."

Will could feel his heartbeat speed up. Something was definitely wrong. The ledger was with him. So, they could not have…

He stilled, for the second time that minute, watching as the page curled, blackened, then caught fire.

If what he was thinking was true, then…

He ran back to the pews, his heart racing wildly. It couldn't be that the Priest had tampered with the ledger. The man sure had no business with the ledger or the Crimson Fist. He was a religious leader, a man of neutral grounds and good character.

He threw open the book and began to flip through the pages, his eyes perusing each page carefully.

The more he flipped, the more allayed his fears became. The pages were still very much intact. He'd been very wrong to think that—

A torn page.

Will blinked once, then twice, noting the rough-line of paper between two sheets of the ledger. Then very slowly, he backed away, legs trembling, stopping only when his legs nearly collided with Mary.

Her eyes fluttered open immediately. "Will?" she whispered.

He shook his head, voice hushed. "The priest... he betrayed us. He's working for them."

Mary sat up, her hands hurrying to clutch her music box. "What? No, why would he do that?"

"I was just there, watching him destroy the sheet," Will ground out, slowly shaking his head, too shocked to comprehend the matter. He could feel himself growing closer to explosion. "I stood right there, allowing myself to be blinded foolishly by trust while he set the sheet ablaze."

"Look, I do not understand any of what you're

saying!" Mary tried to hold his arm but he flinched, his eyes burning with rage.

"Father O'Malley would not touch the ledger. He's not a part of them!" Mary defended.

Will stormed towards the place he'd seen the Priest, the rest of the ledger in his hand. The stranger was now gone. Father O'Malley stood with his back to them, hands behind him, eyes locked on a crucifix nailed to the moss-stained wall before him.

Will hissed under his breath. *Pretender!*

"Explain this, Father!" He spat the revering word sardonically and with great decision. "Three teenagers decide to trust you with just one thing, and you decide to cook up a sabotage while they're asleep?"

Mary pulled the ledger from his hand and flipped through the pages herself, her face still stubborn with disbelief. Perhaps, she thought he had gone bonkers.

But then, in a minute, she discovered herself, her fingers hovering across what was left of the torn page. The Priest had not even tried to be discreet about it. He'd ripped the page very roughly, lie her wanted them to catch him.

O'Malley turned slowly. There was no anger in his face. Only weariness.

"I did," he said. "And I won't lie to you about it."

Mary took on with the charge. "Why?" Incredulousness poured out with her voice. "You knew how much this meant to us! To Will. That ledger could..."

"Could what?" Father O'Malley interrupted, and though his voice remained gentle, there was steel beneath. "Expose monsters? Change the world? Burn London to the ground?"

He stepped closer. "You think I haven't looked through that book? I've seen names in there that hold more power than the Archbishop. Men with smiling portraits and spotless boots, who order beatings with their afternoon tea. You two don't know what you're carrying."

Mary's lips trembled. "Then what you should have done was to help us, and not do something as gruel, behind our backs for that matter!"

"I did what I had to," O'Malley said softly. "That page… it named someone. Someone who still watches this street. Someone with ears in every wall. If it were ever found in this church, there'd be no sanctuary left."

Will's voice broke through. "Who was on it?"

The priest's gaze faltered. He looked away, toward the candlelight flickering against stone. "That's not a name you want to carry."

THE MATCH GIRL

Mary closed the ledger slowly. Her shoulders dropped—not in forgiveness, but exhaustion.

She turned to leave. "We'll go. We've stayed too long."

"No!" Will yelled, red with anger. "Not until he tells us what he took from us!"

O'Malley looked at him, a sorry look melting the resolution in his eyes. "Not now, son. A lot is at stake. The orphans…the church…the sanctuary. If I give you a name, all of those get wrecked, beyond repair."

"A name!" Will felt fire course through his veins. "Otherwise, I'll be forced to do things that will get you speaking sooner or later!"

The priest stared at him quietly for a minute before speaking, his expression still very much collected. "Sir Reginald Pembroke." He glanced at Mary for a second like he wanted to catch her reaction. "You may have heard of him. He's a well respected city magistrate, known publicly for "crusading" against dockside crime."

"Keep talking," Will snapped.

The Priest looked away from them, like he was being inspired by the clear space before him. "All of the stories are façades. The man gets bribed hugely to look the other wayand to send the Constabulary off on wild goose chases whenever the Crimson Fist strikes."

"So, you're saying the paper you destroyed had evidence against him." Will took a big bold step towards him, his hands clenched into tight fists. "You desire to keep his evil deeds hidden and so, you helped him."

"God forbid." O'Malley met his gaze. "I only tore the one page that could invite Pembroke's fury and justify a full-force police raid on the church. I cannot afford to lose my sanctuary or the already tight funding the orphans get monthly."

"That's only a pure display of selfishness and..."

"Get out of here." O'Malley looked at Mary, like she could better understand what he was saying. "The gang knows you're here. There have been whispers of a raid—not from street thugs, but from *official* forces, under orders from higher up. I cannot protect you against them."

"I don't believe anything you've got to say." Will narrowed his eyes at him, his breathing rough and irregular.

"I think we should leave." Mary held his arm lightly, trying to breathe some reason down his neck. "He ha told us the truth."

"You know nothing of the vile and despicable

thing he has done!" He shrugged his arm out of her grip and hid the rest of the ledger deep inside his coat.*He'd not make the mistake of trusting anyone, not anymore.*

The church groaned with the wind.

And then—

A sharp whistle outside.

Not the wind.

Will turned.

Another whistle. Louder. Followed by the sound of heavy boots on stone.

O'Malley stiffened, eyes darting to the side door. "They've found us," he murmured.

A heavy thud struck the wooden doors of the church.

And again.

Will stepped back into the nave, heart pounding.

A voice barked from outside. "Open up! In the name of the law!"

The door hinges groaned.

One more strike…

Boom.

CHAPTER 10

Whoever was after them was surely cheesed off.

They scattered everything; splintering wood and breaking down doors like they were the very earthquake that happened to them. The last time she dared to look back, she'd caught the hot gaze of one of them. He was dressed in uniform, his pursuit too personal to be commanded by the law.

They sure had ties with the Crimson Fist.

Mary ran down the stone steps like she had agun pressed to her spine.*Sods*! That's what they all were.

"Quickly!" Father O'Malley's voice boomed behind her as he yanked a rusted iron lever beneath a carved relief of Saint Jude. Stone ground against stone, and a narrow door creaked open into a wall of choking dust and darkness.

Will moved very fluidly, like he was just cut out for the rough life. At some point, she even became unsure of his newness at running from hot and angry blokes. The chase. The adrenaline. The game of revenge and murder. He seemed to have a penchant for them all.

She almost stilled, under the influence of such thoughts. If something—anything at all—happened to them in the inclines of love, she surely wouldn't be open to taking to her heels every breath and second.

They'd have to grow a family, and it'd sure be on stable grounds and similar mind!

He took her hand just then, like he had heard her thoughts and was trying to reassure her. Her nerves tickled, the heat of his hand smothering hers as he pulled her into the narrow passageway.

"Did Tommy tell you where he went? I didn't see him in the sanctuary."

Her head kicked back into place. *Tommy! What had she been thinking, forgetting him like that?* "I didn't see him either!" Good Lord! The lad never was in one place, and now, she'd be troubled all day, thinking about his whereabouts.

"I'm sure he'll find us. He always does." Will tightened his grip on her hand, his thumb drawing small but reassuring arcs across her skin, even in the heat of it all.

Mary took one last glance behind, hoping for a second that Tommy would appear from somewhere, like he always did. But to her greatest horror, she saw none other than the thieving Constable, first in line, his moves powered strongly by revenge.

The priest ducked in last, slamming the hidden door just as the church above thundered with shouting men and stomping boots.

Mary didn't consider stopping after that. If those men got them—her—she'd be finished.

Their footsteps echoed In the silence of the catacombs.Mary clutched her music box to her chest, her breath sharp and shallow.

The lantern O'Malley carried threw warped shadows across brickwork as old as the city itself. Ancient pipes glistened with damp. Cobwebs laced the ceiling like forgotten lace.

"How far does it go?" Will whispered.

"Far enough," the priest replied, voice low. "This tunnel was built by monks to flee Henry's soldiers. It's outlived fire, plague, and now corruption."

"I don't trust you either," Will murmured, the anger still in his voice.

The priest didn't reply, and for Mary, their gravelly exchange did the least to bother her. Her heartbeat roared louder than their steps. She hated tunnels. They reminded her of the coal holes, the places she'd hid when debt collectors raided tenements. Back then, she'd had no one.

Now—Will's hand was still gripping hers. Warm. Steady.

She held tighter.

Minutes blurred. The tunnel rose and fell in uneven dips. Her boots scraped moss. Finally, the passage narrowed, and Father O'Malley whispered, "We're close."

He pushed open a half-buried grate. Cold night air rushed in, heavy with chimney soot and garden lavender. They climbed into a tangled garden behind a slant-roofed house.

Mary knew it instantly. The stone lions by the birdbath. The crooked washing line.

Mrs. Aldridge's house.

She looked at O'Malley, surprised. "You know Mrs. Aldridge?"

He nodded. "She's a good keeper of the Sanctuary. She has a good heart, that woman."

"What if the soldiers come through this tunnel, looking for us?" Will wouldn't stop looking back.

O'Malley beamed, like their escape was something he'd enjoyed. "They never will find you. It's a maze in there. You only made it through because I followed you. They would only get lost and have their regrets."

"Besides," he continued, "I'll go back to the Sanctuary. They'll settle when they see me."

"They'll arrest you!" Will tried to sound detached, but failed, woefully.

O'Malley patted his back. "They can only wreck me by destroying the orphanage. No one arrests a Minister of Scripture. At least, not Pembroke. He has an odd reverence for men of God."

They walked untoMrs. Aldridge's porch. But before they could knock, the door creaked open. A candle backlit the seamstress, her gray hair pinned up, spectacles catching firelight.

"Mary Fletcher," she murmured, eyeing Will warily. "I see you've brought friends." The distrust in her eyes only whistled away when she saw Father O'Malley. "Father!" She opened the door a bit wider. "Come in, please!"

They stepped inside. It smelled of peppermint and ink.

O'Malley stayed by the door. "I brought them to you because they need your help."

"I know Mary." She hurried to haul a stool for the Priest but the man refused to sit. "I was friends with her Ma."

"They have this ledger." The Priest nodded at Will. "Lay it out here for her to peruse. She cuts through the evil buried in books just as easily as she cuts through fabric."

A blush stained Mrs. Aldridge's cheek. "I left that life to abandonment years ago." She readjusted her spectacles. "Never did me any good. The evil…" Her eyes twinkled with a sadness that spoke volumes of bad history, but it was gone almost immediately.

Willopened the ledger on the kitchen table. The parchment was creased and smudged, but the names glared like lantern light—dock officials, constables, the name Pembroke underlined in fading red.

Mrs. Aldridge adjusted her spectacles again and began scanning. The parlour, lit by a single oil lamp, flickered with shadows that danced across the faded wallpaper.

"Sloppy handwriting, sloppy accounting," she muttered. "But damning."

Will sat across from her, his eyes wary, while Mary remained standing, taut with anticipation.

"I haven't published anything this dangerous in years," she said, her voice sharp, yet not unkind. "I had hoped to die with clean hands. Yet here you are—dragging me back into the mire."

Mary said nothing. She didn't flinch under Aldridge's scrutiny. The woman sure had questions for her. She probably couldn't understand how she'd found herself in the midst of deep-seated evil like the one contained in the ledger.

Perhaps, one day, she'd tell her how she'd done it for love.

With a sigh, Mrs. Aldridge picked up the first page, her finger following a scrawl of ink and numbers. "This one... this is Pembroke's route. Payments for silence. Names I recognise—constables, clerks. Even a doctor or two." Her voice grew quieter. "You understand, don't you, that if this is real, we're all going to be hunted?"

"We already are," Will murmured.

Mrs. Aldridge looked up sharply, her eyes scanning his bruised face. "You're the dock boy. The one who nearly died." She took a step back and began to search her desk frantically for something.

"Anything the matter, Aldridge?" the priest called off, staring at her unsurely.

She finally pulled off a sheet of paper from a

bigger pile. "Here!" She plastered a white sheet to the kitchen counter, just beside the ledger. "A bounty."

Mary leaned in, a gasp tearing through her throat at the sight of Will. Someone had made a pencil drawing of him, the portrait backed up with words in cursive writing.

£20 REWARD

For capture of William Hartley

Dead or Alive

"They want me at all cost."

Mary, ticked off by mad anger picked up the sheet and scrunched it into a ball. "Bastards!"

The Priest looked right at her, her choice of language clearly not sitting well with him. Mary looked away from him, too hot in the head to feel embarrassed. "We have to take the longer stride, be at the top of this darn game!"

"Miss Fletcher!" Father O'Malley called, a frown knitting the lines across face together. "Do not let your anger guide your tongue down the wrong lanes!"

"If we release this out there," Will pushed the ledger back to everyone's focus. "Will people believe it's real?"

"Some will," Mrs. Aldridge answered. "But we need Pembroke's personal ledger. His handwriting, his seal. This copy might be enough for whispers, not war." She continued to flip through the pages of the ledger. "If this book is as dangerous as they say, then, it sure has something we can use."

O'Malley cleared his throat. "I burned it."

Mrs. Aldridge's gaze snapped to him, her ears tipping forward like she'd heard wrong. "You what?"

"Don't look at me like Iburned the whole book," he said, calm but unrepentant. "One page. One that tied back to the orphans. To the church."

"And you thought that gave you the right—?" Will started.

"Don't pretend you know what I've seen," the priest said. His voice didn't rise, but it cut like a blade. "Children sold for coin. Bought off books like grain or flour. If that page survived, the gang wouldn't just destroy this church—they'd drag every orphan with it. They'd hang me in the square and use the rest for firewood."

Will stood, fury flashing in his eyes. "So you made the choice for us all."

"I made the choice to protect the ones I could," O'Malley said, folding his hands. "Even if it cost me your trust."

The room stilled.

Mary's eyes burned, but her voice was gentle. "You should've told us."

"Perhaps," he murmured. "But you were barely breathing, and he was still bleeding. Forgive me if I didn't want to hand our last chance at justice to Pembroke's men with a neat red ribbon."

Mrs. Aldridge, who had been silent through the exchange, finally sighed. "We can't print with this."

Mary looked up, heart sinking. "But..."

"I believe it," Aldridge said, lifting the papers. "But belief doesn't make a headline stick. If we're to expose Pembroke, we need more than names and numbers. We need his signature. Ink, wax, blood if necessary."

"But the page he signed is gone," Mary whispered. She hated to think of the consequence of whatever she was saying.

A chair creaked by the window.

"Not all of them," came a voice.

They turned.

Tommy stepped in from the dark threshold like a ghost come home. Damp and grinning, eyes rimmed red with exhaustion.

Mary stared, too excited and shocked to move an inch towards him. "Tommy?" She'd envisioned grabbing him by the collar, screaming a warning into his ears, and many other not too pleasant things. But now, she just couldn't...

"Oh heavens! The sacredness of my home has sure been violated."

"I had to leave before dawn." Tommy kept his gaze on her. "Didn't want to wake your friend—not when he'd finally stopped bleeding all over the floor."

"How did you find me?" She took one small step forward, her lips still parted in shock.

He grinned sheepishly, his face smudged with soot. "Knew I'd find you here. You only ever trusted two people—him and her." He pointed at the Priest and then, Mrs. Aldridge. "Now, I have to get used to adding the new lad to the list." He chuckled a little. "A mighty expansion, you agree?"

Will's face tightened. He didn't seem a bit pleased. "Why didn't you come with us?" He eyed Tommy's muddy boots. "Where did you scurry off to?"

"I had to check something," he said. "To be sure I could do what you'd need next."

Mrs. Aldridge narrowed her eyes. "And what, pray tell, is that?"

Tommy pulled out a crumpled scrap of paper and unfolded it. A charcoal rubbing—imperfect, blurred

—but it bore the unmistakable looping P of Pembroke's signature.

"I peeked in the magistrate's window last night," he said. "Saw his big ledger sitting by the fire—wide open. He signs it every day. Page after page. Sloppy as sin."

"How did you know about the Magistrate?" Will took two big steps towards him, his eyes drilling through Tommy's, the air in the room buzzing alongside with hardcore tension. "You haven't been here. Yet, you know about him, the signature, everything." A nerve ticked in his jaw. "Who do you think you hold by your foolery?"

"You think I haven't been watching Pembroke all these months? I've heard whispers in alleyways—about how he keeps a private ledger. How every dirty constable and crooked judge has their name scribbled in it."

Will folded his arms, watching him. "So you just took off into the night to break into the magistrate's house on a hunch?"

If Tommy was hurt by Will's incessant drill, he didn't show it. "I was going to tell you about Pembroke when I saw you with the ledger. But after all that happened yesterday, I needed to be sure. I needed to watch him and in turn, know his plans."

"Then, the signature? How did you know of that?"

Tommy sighed. "I overheard your argument with the Priest while I tried to break in. It only made me remember what I'd seen. Which is why I'm offering to help."

Mrs. Aldridge leaned forward, still studying the rubbing. "Well, this is a start. A good one," she said. Then her eyes moved to Tommy's. "Would you go back?"

He shrugged. "Give me a scarf and a biscuit. I've been in worse places than a magistrate's office. Besides… they never change the locks. Not for street rats like me."

Mary's chest tightened. He was younger than her by a year, yet walked like he'd lived through ten wars.

She touched his arm. "You sure?"

"This ledger—it changes everything." For the first time in a long time, an earnest expression sat on his face, his nose wrinkling. "Whitechapel gets a new life. I want to be part of it."

"That's too much risk," the priest muttered. "If he ever gets caught…"

"I believe it's wrong to sit still," Mary said. She held up the scrunched up ball in her hand. "See this?

Time is ticking, and if we continue to run away from harm's way, they'll have Will's head." A grimace tore through her face as she gave more thought to her words.

Mrs. Aldridge stood. "Then we move quickly." She shot Tommy a pointed look. "I'll see your truth in every newspaper from Whitechapel to Westminster, once you get the signature."

"You have my word."

Mary watched as Tommy slipped into the dark like a shadow, his torn coatflying behind him like two tongues. She forced herself to sit, letting her bones thaw.

Will slid into the chair beside her."You believed in him." His voice was barely above a whisper.

"You didn't?" She met his gaze, trying to read through those mysterious orbs.

"I do now," he admitted. "Because you did."

She looked down, smiling faintly. "He's rough, but his heart's cleaner than most."

Outside, from the street, came the sharp whistle of a constable's warning—and the rumble of hooves drawing close.Mrs. Aldridge turned toward the window, the flame of the lamp catching in her eyes.

"Oh God," she whispered. "I think they've found us."

Mary's eyes snapped to the window.

A black carriage rolled into view, torches flanking it. Pembroke. His face pale and furious through the glass. Behind him, mounted officers dismounted.

Mary stared as the magistrate's boots hit the gravel, imagining how a man could be so despicably cruel.

Father O'Malley's face turned grim. "He knows."

Will moved to the back door. Mary grabbed the ledger, her heart hammering again.

The knock came—sharp, commanding.

Mrs. Aldridge extinguished the candle. "No one says a word."

CHAPTER 11

The knock came again, harder this time. Not frantic, not desperate. Just firm. A sound that carried authority. Will stiffened where he stood, instinctively placing himself between Mary and the door, though there was little he could do barehanded.

Mrs. Aldridge didn't flinch. She smoothed her skirt and raised her chin. "I know Pembroke well enough," she said quietly, her voice edged in steel. "He wouldn't come alone."

"Should we open?" Mary whispered, her voice shaky.

"No," Mrs. Aldridge said. "And we don't speak."

Outside, Pembroke's voice carried. Calm. Eerily composed.

"Mrs. Aldridge," he called, "you've been quiet for years. Now suddenly, your lights burn through the night." He let out a predatory chuckle, like he couldn't believe her guts. "Old ghosts creeping out of your pressroom, perhaps?" He knocked again, the poor wooden door trembling beneath the force.

"I suggest you open up. Before we're forced to assume the worst."

Will's fists clenched. The man didn't even have proof—just a threat wrapped in silk.

Yet it rattled the air like thunder.

Perhaps, it was why Father O'Malley was so terrified of him. Even now, the man had gone pallid in the face.

A beat passed.

Then another knock, though lighter. More of a test than a demand.

Mrs. Aldridge moved to the wall and pressed her hand flat against the paneling. "Follow me," she mouthed, nodding to the rest of them. She opened a cabinet, revealing a narrow staircase that led downward into the depths of the annex. "This way. The pressroom's back entrance opens onto the alley."

"Do you think he knows we're here?" Father O'Malley asked in a low tone.

"He suspects," she replied. "But he has no proof—yet. Let's keep it that way."

They moved swiftly through the cramped passage, Mary brushing Will's arm as they ducked into the tunnel. The narrowness forced them close—he could hear her breath catch as the stair creaked beneath them.

Outside, Pembroke's voice rang out one last time.

"You've made your choice, Aldridge. I won't wait long."

"He's terrified." Mrs. Aldridge scoffed. "He never delivers his message himself. Always sends someone, acting like he's King of the Jungle." Pride floated alongside her words, a little anger sparking off at the edges. "A little brush of fire here and there, and now, he comes running out, his tail dancing behind him."

They emerged into a narrow corridor choked with cobwebs and the scent of old paper. Mrs. Aldridge moved ahead, her lantern casting long shadows on the walls. At the end of the hall, she unlocked a heavy wooden door and pushed it open with effort. The hinges groaned like something woken from a long sleep.

"You really wrapped things up," Father O'Malley murmured, his hand swatting away thecobwebs before his face.

"Tailoring and garment joining appeals more to the sane part of me."

Will stepped in, drawn by the large space before them.

The pressroom lay still, draped in layers of dust and thicker cobwebs. Sheets of brittle newsprint lay scattered on the floor, their edges curling with age.

Will turned around, catching sight of the handpress that stood in the centre of the room, a monument forgotten by time—its levers stiff with rust, the tray half-filled with cracked type blocks.

Mary coughed lightly. "You used to run this?"

Mrs. Aldridge set the lantern down. "Before the threats, yes.The last piece I published nearly cost me my life." Her voice carried no bitterness, only memory. "But it's still here." She patted the handpress, a wistful expression on her face. "And we'll make it sing again."

Will ran his hand over the press's side, lifting a veil of dust that clung to his fingertips like ash. "It'll need work."

"We'll manage," Mrs. Aldridge said. "You two"—she gestured to Will and Mary—"can start cleaning the rollers and sorting the usable type. I'll find the ink and oil."

"And, what…what about the crew?" Mary stuttered, looking somewhat overwhelmed by the volume work that stretched across them.

Will smiled, only a little, amused by the fear that was beginning to make its way into her eyes.

"There is no crew." Mrs. Aldridge gave her a tired smile. "They're gone. Married. Dead. Afraid." She shrugged. "Take your pick. If we want this truth printed, we'll have to do it ourselves."

Will grabbed a broom from the corner. "You don't have to do anything." He shot her a smile. "I know you don't want to.

She gulped, blinking rapidly at the same time, like she'd been caught doing the wrong thing. "You're in the wrong." She grabbed a broom too. "I clean for a living. You don't know that!"

He nodded, growing all the more amused.

"Stop looking at me like that!" She pointed the broom at him, her eyes narrowing.

"How?" he joked, really struggling to keep his laughter down. Now was neither the time…nor the place.

She tucked a curl of her beautiful dark hair behind her ear. "You know how you're looking at me." Her face turned red. "Goodness, rid your face of that sly smile you have on."

"We should hurry," Father O'Malley muttered,

throwing them a disapproving glare. "We have hours, not days."

"I've never worked a typewriter before." Mary looked even more exhausted just by staring at the old dusty machine. "And I'm guessing by the puzzled looks on everyone's faces that we allare ignoramuses, with little to no experience." She looked at Mrs. Aldridge, like she hoped to appeal to the soft side of her. "So, in my opinion, if we indeed have little time, we'd better get help."

"You'll learn," Mrs. Aldridge said, not a bit dispirited. "Everyone pulls their weight. Even priests." She turned to Father O'Malley, who gave a reluctant nod and rolled up his sleeves.

"Oh well…" Mary muttered.

They worked quickly, sweat dampening their brows despite the morning chill. Will learned to ink the rollers. Mary cleaned the movable type with a rag, each letter block revealing itself like a small miracle.

Mrs. Aldridge moved among them, giving instructions with the kind of precision that came from muscle memory—though her hands shook slightly at first.

"I can't believe it's working," Mary whispered as the machine creaked into motion.

Will forced himself to focus on something else other than her face, which was now illuminated with so much pride. She would let out a tiny little squeal each time the machine printed a letter and his heart would jump in response.

He could even spend the entire day watching her and not tire.

Good Lord.

"The machine is not yet in full swing," Mrs. Aldridge replied, in her elements, her face brighter than when she was handling fabric. "But it will."

As the press started rolling, the rhythmic clanking and whirring of the machine seemed to shake off the years of silence. The first test print came off the rollers, the letters dark and crisp on the page. Mrs. Aldridge inspected it, nodding In satisfaction.

"Good," she murmured, her voice barely above the hum of the press. "Now, let's do this properly."

The scent of ink filled the room as they set to work. Will watched Mrs. Aldridge expertly place the printed sheets, her hands steady despite the chaos of the situation. For the first time in days, the air felt alive with purpose.

Mrs. Aldridge had stationed him to the press. His hands, now soiled with ink,moved with a confidence he had never known before. And for the first time since he began the chase, he felt himself enjoy it all—the slow, deliberate process of creation amidst the turmoil of their lives.

His eyes kept flicking to Mary, who was standing at a worktable across from him, sorting fresh sheets of printed paper into neat piles, her head slowly bobbing to the song she hummed.

She glanced at him and smiled faintly, a small flicker of warmth in the hard space between them. It wasn't much, but it was enough.

The first copies rolled hot from the press, the ink still gleaming wet in the pale morning light. Will caught one as it dropped into the basket, and for a moment, he simply stared.

The headline screamed in bold black type:

Magistrate Pembroke and the Web of Blood Money

Exclusive: Names of Inspectors, Constables, and Merchants on the Take

Smaller headlines ran just below.

Ledger Pages Reveal Kill List—11 Names Crossed Out

Mrs. Aldridge skimmed the copy as Will handed it to her. She gave a quiet nod. "It's good," she said. "Too good for them to ignore." Her voice cracked slightly—an echo of the old fire returning to her after years away from the ink.

"How do we get the paper out?" Father O'Malley asked, wiping sweat off his brow. His white robe had now grown the lightest shade of brown, but he didn't seem to mind much.

"We don't need to do anything." Mrs. Aldridge grabbed some of the sheets and balanced them on her arm. "The sound of the mills surely announced us." She tugged at the blinds gently, her eyes perusing the fields. "I've caught a couple curious eyes staring through the window."

She turned the locks in the door before tugging at the handle, the light from outside pouring into the room in silvery lines. "The world is hungry for news. They'll come for it, like any to sugar."

A few neighbourhood boys—one barefoot, one too small for his father's coat—arrived first, drawn by the hum of the press and the promise of coin. Mrs. Aldridge pressed three copies into their hands with a sharp whisper. "Go. Spread the news."

Others came—an old man with a basket who used to sell apples, a mute seamstress who took a bundle with wide eyes and noddedonce before slipping out the back gate.

Mary helped organize the leaflets by street name,

marking routes with chalk on the floor. "Don't leave too many in one place," she warned. "They'll burn them."

She seemed very skilled with her chore, dishing each person some advice to run with. Will watched her with warmth pooling in his chest as she laughed with a dockworker.

He stepped outside as the first true crowd began to gather. At first, they came in twos and threes—dockhands rubbing sleep from their eyes, shop boys on morning errands, a maid with ink on her apron who must've already found a copy.

Then soon enough, a stir grewfrom them, culminating slowly into loud murmurs and complaints.

"Latham? I know the man. He takes rent on East Gate."

"And Samuels—he collects for Pembroke's office."

"My cousin saw them drag that girl down Fair Brook Alley last month…"

The murmurs grew louder. Heads nodded. Others turned red with fury. Someone read a paragraph aloud about the grain inspectors falsifying safety certificates.

A market vendor gasped, then tore the page and pinned it to her stall.

Mary moved through them quietly, slipping one

leaflet into the hand of a gray-bearded dockworker who had stood silent for a long while. He read it. Then folded it once, tucked it inside his coat, and pressed his fingers over it as though it were a letter from home.

Will watched from the stoop before falling in step with Mary. "You're not scared?"

"I am," she said softly, watching the old man walk away. "But not enough to stop."

He felt the heat of her presence more acutely than ever in that moment. All of the useful milestones they'd ticked off, where they currently stood,everything, was only possible because of her invaluable input. She'd connected all the dots, brought in all her friends, all in chase of a fight she had no business in.

"Are you sure about this?" Will asked quietly as she handed another paper over.

Mary met his gaze, her expression a mixture of fear and defiance. "We have no choice, Will. We have to make them see. This..." she held up one of the leaflets, her fingers tracing the edge like it might shatter at the slightest touch, "this is the only way to make it stop."

He wanted to say more—so many things—but the press clanged again, and behind them, Aldridge's shout rang out: "Final run! We print until they come through that door."

Will walked back in, only to see that someone else had joined in. The man had a dark look in his eyes, occasionally glancing nervously over his shoulder like he was terrified someone would catch sight of him.

Will's instinct flared, but before he could make a move, Mrs. Aldridge's hand rested lightly on his arm. "It's okay," she said quietly. "He's one of mine."

Will held his tongue but watched as the man approached Mrs. Aldridge. They exchanged a look, and Will noted the subtle, almost imperceptible nod from Aldridge before the man disappeared toward the back.

"He's an informant," Mrs. Aldridge muttered, in response to the curious gazes they all shot her.

Will nodded, albeit slowly. With time, he was getting to discover that she wasn't just an innocent seamstress-turned-journalist. She was playing a dangerous game, weaving threads between the city's elite and the forgotten workers of the docks.

But again, if her carefully crafted allianceswere his only chancesat survival, he'd be sure to embrace them.

As the day wore on, Will's gaze kept finding

Mary in the cluttered pressroom, moving between tables, handing out prints, her every action filled with purpose.

There was a determination in her steps, a strength that had blossomed over the last few days—she was no longer just the frightened girl from the streets. She was becoming a force in her own right.

"You did well," he said, his voice rough from the endless hours of work.

Mary looked up, a flicker of gratitude in her eyes. She opened her mouth to say something, but then—out of nowhere—the sound of a carriage wheel cracked the silence outside the pressroom. The rhythmic pounding of hooves echoed, too close, too deliberate.

Will's heart skipped in his chest. The quiet hiss of the press didn't mask the low murmur of conversation outside. Mrs. Aldridge looked toward the window, her expression hardening.

"Get down," she ordered, her voice low but commanding.

The press continued rolling in the background as everyone ducked low, instinctively hiding behind the heavy, creaking press or in the shadows of the room. Mrs. Aldridge moved to the window, her face pressed against the cold glass as her eyes scanned the street outside.

"Pembroke's carriage," she murmured, her face paling. "He's back, and he's got the constables with him."

Will let out a shaky sigh when he caught sight of the man marching to the porch. This time, he didn't knock the door. He tore right through, his feet jamming hard against the wood.

"Under authority of the magistrate!" a constable roared as batons hit the ground like war drums. "This press is shut down!"

Mrs. Aldridge tire out from the shadows, her eyes ablaze with protective instincts. She climbed atop a crate, voice fierce. "Protect the papers!"

CHAPTER 12

The door crashed open with a force that reverberated through the pressroom like the crack of thunder. Mary's heart stuttered in her chest.If Pembroke was really who Father O'Malley said he was, then they sure were doomed. At least, the papers they'd shared that morning made sure of that. The man had made all headlines, his evil deeds stringed to his name.

"It's okay," Will comforted her by the side, his own voice tinged with a dot of fear too. "It doesn't end here, I promise."

Pembroke's voice, oily and thick with authority, sliced through the air, cold and commanding."Under the authority of the magistrate, I hereby order this press shut down." He kicked at the pail containing the ink jars, annoyance fuelling his moves. "I want all documents seized."

The constables that followed him into the room were an echo of his intent. They were hard-eyed, grim-faced, and armed with batons. They stood in a loose line behind Pembroke, their sharp gazes moving over the room, scanning the space for anything suspicious that threatened their master's control.

Mary's pulse raced in her ears as she pressed herself against the far wall of the room, hidden in the shadows. The sight of Constables that many only reminded her of the night she'd found Will in the gutter.

They'd definitely not forgive her if they found her now. Not that thieving Constable at least.

She caught Will's eye, and for a brief moment, the world seemed to slow. She could see the questions in his face. What now? What should we do?

She shook her head helplessly at him, praying quietly for some kind of miracle. There was no running away now. They were boxed and all surrounded, by the very man who wanted the ledger gone.

The very man they'd cried about to the world in print.

"I knew they'd come." Regret oozed with the priest's words. "Pembroke is a thorough man. You cannot start a storm without getting his feathers ruffled."

Mary refused to be infected by his palpable fear. She directed her gaze instead to Mrs. Aldridge who stood in front of the press, her back straight, her face as unmoving as a statue. She wasn't intimidated. There was no fear in her eyes, only the calm resolve of someone who knew the fight wasn't over.

Pembroke's sneer deepened as he stepped further into the room. "I see you've been busy, Aldridge." His hot gaze swept across the room in one wave. "Printing seditious lies, stirring the muck of corruption." He met her gaze, head on. "I should remind you. You aren't above the law."

His words felt like a slap but Mrs. Aldridge didn't flinch. Instead, she clasped her hands behind her back, her gaze meeting his without hesitation. "You don't get to decide what's true, Pembroke. And you certainly don't get to shut down the truth."

For a moment, no one moved.

The silence was thick, pregnant with the weight of their unspoken words. Mary could feel the heat rising in her chest. She knew Pembroke well enough to understand that words alone wouldn't stop him.

But Mrs. Aldridge was enough to hold him at bay, at least for now.

"You've made your point," Mrs. Aldridge continued, her voice low, but steady. "But you won't find what you're looking for here." She began to pick up the bottles of ink he'd kicked to the side, the fury clear in her moves.

Pembroke's brow furrowed, his eyes narrowing in suspicion. "What are you hiding?" he demanded, stepping closer. "Where are the documents? The ones you've printed?" He kicked at another pail of supplies, a sneer twisting his facial features. "I demand a response!"

The room held its breath.

Aldridge rose to her feet, her hand brushing the edge of the press. "I haven't hidden anything." She eyed the supplies that were now scattered about the floor. "And I assure you. You'll find no records here. No proof of your so-called lies." Her lips curled into something akin to a smile, though it held no warmth. "You're only wasting your time, Pembroke."

Pembroke's eyes darted to the men standing behind him. His voice dropped to a dangerous whisper. "If you won't give me the papers willingly, I'll take them from you. By force, if necessary."

Aldridge didn't even blink. "Do what you must. It won't change a thing."

Before anyone could react, a subtle movement in the back of the room caught Mary's eye. A figure emerged from the shadows—slim, sure-footed, with an air of quiet menace.

Tommy!

Mary's breath caught in her throat. How in Pete's name had he slipped in unnoticed?

He met her gaze for the briefest of seconds, a flicker of something unreadable crossing his face. Then, without a word, he moved swiftly toward Mrs. Aldridge, his steps light but purposeful. His presence cut through the tension like a knife through butter, and for the briefest of moments, Mary felt a strange kind of relief.

He was back.

Tommy was back.

Aldridge gave him a small nod of acknowledgment, her expression unreadable. "I thought you'd be back sooner," she muttered, her voice barely audible. "Did you get it?"

Tommy's lips twitched into a tight, almost imperceptible smile. "I got it."

He reached into his coat pocket and withdrew a small, leather pouch. He held it up for Mrs. Aldridge, who took it from him with a quiet murmur of thanks. She glanced down, her face hardening as she saw what was inside.

Mary didn't need to ask. They'd gotten Pembroke's signature. The one thing they needed to make the publication legal, to ensure their story could see the light of day without further interference.

Pembroke's eyes locked onto the pouch with an unsettling intensity. His lips twisted into a snarl. "What's this?" he spat. He looked back into her eyes. "What are you playing at, Aldridge? You're out of time. The magistrate's orders..."

He said a lot of things but Aldridge wasn't listening. Her voice was ice-cold as she spoke, not giving him the satisfaction of any further attention. "You're too late, Pembroke. The truth has already been printed, and it's out of your hands."

He stepped forward, his mouth opening in protest, only for the sound of his voice to be drowned by the resounding crash of the back door slamming open. Pembroke turned sharply, his gaze flicking to the constables standing guard. They moved quickly, stepping into position, their hands reaching for their batons.

Mrs. Aldridge stepped in front of the press, her

body a shield. "I'll handle this," she said firmly, not breaking her stance. "You all get out. Quickly."

"Mrs. Aldridge..." Will started, but she silenced him with a sharp shake of her head.

"Go," she urged, her eyes hard. "You won't be able to help me now. Go. Get out with the papers. I'll catch up."

Tommy's hand gripped Will's arm, a quiet command to follow. "She's right. Let's go."

Mary hesitated for a moment, her heart aching at the thought of leaving Aldridge behind, but the urgency in Tommy's voice left no room for argument. They moved toward the back, quietly slipping into the narrow passage hidden behind the press.

Mrs. Aldridge stood firm, her gaze never leaving Pembroke as he advanced. "This isn't over," she said softly, but there was a weight to her words. "I'll be back for the rest."

The others didn't look back as they fled through the corridor, their footsteps muffled in the dust-ridden passage. The oppressive silence of the hidden alley greeted them like a cold embrace, and for a moment, they just stood there, catching their breath.

Mrs. Aldridge's parting words lingered in Mary's mind.

I'll be back for the rest.

They had to return for her. One way or the other.

Tommy turned to Will and Mary, his expression grim. "We'll make sure she's not alone in this. Besides, the Priest is in there with her. She'll be fine." He shot her an impatient look. "We need to move fast, Mary."

They turned a corner into a quiet, narrow street at the back of the building. The heavy pressroom door remained locked, sealing in the noise and chaos. But Mary knew it wouldn't be long before Pembroke and his men followed them out.

They were the most relentless men she'd ever come across in her entire life!

"Where now?" Will asked, his voice tight with urgency.

Tommy didn't answer immediately. His eyes flicked to the alley ahead, alert to every sound, every movement. He motioned for them to keep moving. "We have to find someplace to regroup."

They hurried through the darkened streets, the sound of hooves on cobblestones reaching their ears. Mary shivered involuntarily. That was unmistakably the clatter of a mounted patrol.

Pembroke's men again were on the chase, and they were coming fast.

Too fast.

Mary almost crashed to the floor, sick with all the adrenaline. *How were those blokes ever not tired?*

The sound of hooves clattering against the cobblestones grew louder, scaring the daylight out of her.

"It'll end soon, I promise." Will shot her a contrite look. "I'm sorry for bringing you into this."

"This is not about you," she gushed. "This is for a much bigger cause…a change. I'm only glad to be a part of it."

She was far from glad!

Her lungs burned like someone had buried coal stones in them, and she couldn't even stop running to catch her breath.

Damn!

Tommywas the only one who still looked calm, making quick, calculated movements that led them into a narrow passage, the walls pressing in on all sides. Mary squinted against the dark, the flickering gaslights from the streetcasting long and sharp shadows that seemed to follow them.

"We just have to keep moving," Tommy muttered, his voice tight with urgency. His eyes were darting back and forth, scanning the street ahead and trying also to measure the distance they had to their advantage.

Mary pressed onward, her footsteps quick and muffled against the damp stones.

Only that for some sick reason, the sound of those hooves was unmistakable, growing closer. Louder.

It wasn't even just one rider anymore—they'd grown into a group, a patrol.

"Darn those Constables!" she screamed, out of breath, hoping they at least heard her.

She had only barely gotten over the horror of the resounding and nearing hooves when a figure, tall and cloaked in darkness, stepped out from the shadow of a narrow doorway ahead of them.

Mary froze, the sight of the figure sending a cold wave of dread through her body. The figure didn't move, didn't speak—just stood there, almost like a sentinel in the murk.

"We have to move faster," Tommy hissed under his breath. His voice was strained, but controlled. He nodded toward the alley's far end, where a darkened street continued into the blackness. "Now."

But Mary's eyes were locked on the figure, her heart pounding so loudly she thought it might give them away.

"There they are!"

The shriek tore her attention from the still

figure. The clattering of hooves had stopped. All that was left was a man's voice, gruff and commanding.

"Just around the bend!"

Tommy's face hardened, his eyes flicking over to the dark figure in front of them. He cursed softly under his breath. "We've been made. Run!"

The mounted patrol was getting closer, and their heavy boots were now pounding on the cobblestones. There were more voices now, shouting, calling orders. The patrol wasn't just looking for them—they were closing in, fast.

Tommy took a step back, his eyes flashing with the weight of a decision. "I'll hold them off. Get to the next street."

Mary's pulse spiked, and her chest tightened. "Tommy, no!"

He didn't answer. In one smooth motion, he spun on his heel, drawing his coat tighter around him. Without looking back, he darted toward the figure, disappearing into the shadows. A fleeting glance told her it was the figure that moved first, not Tommy.

Bile rose in her throat.

Had they been waiting for him?

"Go!" Tommy shouted, his voice distant now, blending with the night as he disappeared into the darkness.

Will grabbed her arm, pulling her forward. "We don't have time!" His grip was firm, his voice full of the urgency that she felt in every fibre of her being.

The clattering hooves and shouts were nearly upon them. The patrol had spotted Tommy's diversion, but they hadn't seen them yet.

It was their last chance to escape.

Will's eyes met hers with a fierce determination. "We can't help him now. We need to move."

Mary didn't argue. They pushed forward, running through the alley, the sound of their footsteps drowned out by the pounding hooves of the patrol behind them. They had no time to look back.

But as they reached the next corner, a shout rang through the night—sharp and angry.

"Stop them!"

A rider, leaning low in his saddle, appeared at the end of the alley, his hand gripping a baton. Her heart skipped a beat. No, two.

The mounted patrol was closing in! They rounded the corner, but the streets ahead seemed darker, the path narrowing with each breath.

The patrol was upon them.

Mary's breath hitched in her throat, the adrenaline coursing through her veins. The chase was on.

Their lives—everything they had fought for—hung in the balance, with no guarantee of escape.

And Tommy… he was still back there, somewhere in the night, facing Pembroke's men alone.

The sound of the hooves grew louder.

And louder.

It was now or never.

CHAPTER 13

They had to keep moving. They had to get away.

Tommy had sacrificed himself. Mrs. Aldridge and the Priest too. It'd be too bad for them to get caught.

The streets were narrow and dark, the night air thick with the scent of damp stone and the whisper of hurried feet. Will's breath came in shallow gasps as he pulled Mary along through the winding alleys, the sound of galloping hooves too close for comfort.

"Keep going, Mary!" Will urged, his voice ragged. "We have to get to the docks. We can board a boat there."

Mary's face was pale, eyes wide with fear, but her feet never faltered. The streets blurred in Will's vision as they rounded another corner, ducking into the shadow of an old warehouse. His pulse was a thrum in his ears. He could almost feel the horses' breath on his neck.

"Will," Mary gasped, "they're gaining. What if they—?"

"We won't let them catch us. Just trust me," he replied, his tone harder than he felt. The moment the words left his mouth, he knew he had to keep her safe.

He couldn't let them win. He wouldn't.

As they dashed through another alley, a new sound broke through the chase—the sharp crack of a baton against stone. The constables were getting closer, closer than ever before. Will's heart raced faster, each beat a drum of impending disaster.

"Go left!" he hissed, pointing toward a narrow gap between two crumbling buildings. "I'll split from you. I'll double back, meet you at the safe house."

Her eyes flitted to him, panic flaring. "No, Will! Don't..."

"I'll be fine," he interrupted. "Trust me."

There was no time. He needed her safe.

Mary hesitated, then nodded, her face pale with a mixture of fear and resolve. "Just come back. Promise me."

"I will," he said, forcing the words through

clenched teeth, and then, without another moment's hesitation, he veered to the left, weaving into the shadows.

She didn't look back. And neither did he.

Will darted through the alleyways, his body coiled with tension. His breath ragged in his chest, the heat of the chase still burning in his veins. He had to lose them, to give Mary time to get away. His footsteps echoed, and he quickened his pace, heart hammering in his chest.

But then, as fate would have it, his luck ran out. A rough hand gripped his arm from the shadows, pulling him into a darkened corner. Will barely had time to react before he found himself face-to-face with the enemy—

"Will!"

"Tommy?" Will gasped, surprised, his mind still racing from the pursuit.

Tommy's face was grim, his eyes hard with something Will couldn't quite place. Bruises marred his cheek, and his clothes were torn in places. But somehow, he was right there—alive, breathing.

"Tommy!" This time, his voice oozed thickly with relief.

"Thought you might need help," Tommy

muttered, his voice low. "I wasn't far behind you." He glanced into the darkness briefly. "Where's Mary?"

"She's at the docks. I had to distract the Constables so that she could run safely without them on her trail." Will blinked, confusion clouding his thoughts still. "How did you—?"

The Constables rode past just then, stirring along with them a blanket of dust and noise.

"I don't know how much longer we can keep this up, Will." He ran a hand through his hair, eyes darting to the shadows. "Pembroke's men are everywhere, even among the constables. I barely slipped past them."

Will stood still for a moment, the weight of their situation settling over him like a dark cloud. He had thought they were alone in this fight, that the danger was manageable—but Tommy's words only reminded him of the truth.

Pembroke was more dangerous than they had ever imagined.

"Tommy, we..."

"Not now," Tommy interrupted, lowering his voice. He looked down at the small bundle of papers he'd been clutching. "Mrs. Aldridge sent a note."

He handed it to Will, who tore it open with trembling fingers. The words inside were brief but clear:

They know you're in the city.

We need to act quickly. Someone who might be able to help is waiting. A friend of Pembroke's past—he could be the key.

Wait at my Safe house. It's just behind the creek.

Will stared at the note, his heart pounding with both fear and determination. "We have to find this ally," he said. "It's our only shot."

Tommy nodded. "That's why I'm here." He peered through the dark corner. "We've lost the Constables. Let's find Mary."

* * *

THEY FOUND Mary by the docks, her small body weaving out of the tall grass the moment she caught sight of them.

She was safe.

Will let out an exhale he didn't even realize he'd been holding. Thank goodness.

She was safe!

"Will," she cried, her voice laced with relief. "You're alright!" She made an attempt to embrace him, but stopped herself in time, her arms falling back to her side limply.

He nodded, stepping forward to take her arm,

struggling to keep his disappointment at bay. *An embrace would have surely lifted his spirits.*

"I promised, didn't I?"

Her eyes flickered for a moment with something softer, but it quickly faded, her attention snapping towards Tommy. "Tommy, you too!"

Tommy smirked at her. "Don't get all weepy now, Miss Fletcher. I'm hale and hearty!"

She slapped his arm playfully. "I was so certain I would die a few minutes back. You don't know how relieved I feel!"

Will watched as they exchanged more of their friendly banter, his cheeks flaming hot. Tommy sure looked very much ecstatic, the urgency of the matter at hand buried somewhere at the back of his mind.

"We need to get to Mrs. Aldridge's safe house." His voice came out roughly—more than he'd intended. But at least, it did the job of getting their attention back.

"Safe house?" Mary asked tiredly, like she was starting to get bored of the entire thing.

"Mrs. Aldridge sent a letter. She wants us to wait there."

He began to march forward, still annoyed by them. Behind him, they continued their banter, slapping their arms playfully and making more funny sounds.

Will scoffed, wiling himself to focus on something else. The streets were now alive with whispers of their escape, and that made him uncomfortable. Pembroke's influence was spreading through every layer of the city, and now, even the constables had been compromised.

It wasn't just about getting away anymore—it was about fighting back.

They arrived at the safe house deep into the night, the structure too similar to Mary's old theatre. It was old, yet the warmth wrapped them to the toes. His gaze wandered again to Mary. She'd lost too much, all for him, and sometimes, he wondered if she realized.

He had nothing, but then, every second, he found himself wanting to reassure her of a future—their future. He'd be by her side, his arms wrapped tightly around her and his lips whispering sweet promises into her ear. Then, maybe they'd dance to the song she always hummed, their laughter rocking the wind.

He clenched his jaws painfully, his heart thrumming in longing—a sharp desire that almost startled him. She was checking through the cabinets for some candles, the moonlight the only thing that guided her fingers. He moved closer to her, his heartbeat rising with each step.

"Did you find any yet?"

She jumped, and would have crashed to the floor had he not hurried to catch her, his eyes wide. "I didn't realize you'd be startled." He gulped, trying not to think too much of her proximity. "I apologize."

She let out a nervous chuckle, her hands shaking against his chest. "One can never know what to expect these days."

He was going to respond with his own nervous laugh, but then, the sound died somewhere along his throat, leaving him to stare at her, lips parted and dumbstruck. *How could still she be so pretty even after they'd only just survived hell and death?* Her eyes—they shone like silvery dots beneath the moonlight, her lips softly inviting, calling, whispering...

A shiver danced down his spine.

"Mary." This time, her name tumbled out of his lips with need—a longing he'd kept hidden from her perusal.

He'd wanted a perfect time...or maybe a perfect place. Roses. Sunshine. But now, with her body melting under his touch, he just couldn't hold back, not for another second. He tightened his grip around her waist, drawing her closer to himself. "I asked you a question the other day."

She didn't blink or move. She just stared right back at him, probably locked in the same web as he was.

"Are you betrothed to someone?" He pulled her a little closer, too hungry for her touch—all of it.

Her breathing went from zero to hundred within the second, her hot breath stirring up every nerve in him.

"Why...why do you ask?" Her voice was small, locked tightly in a whisper.

He closed his eyes for a second and breathed her in, the pleasure rocking all the way to his feet. "I have been taken by you, my lady." He released her a little, hoping that she'd not feel too compelled. What he wanted was a response birthed from the most natural depths. "I know the timing is unfit and that the..."

"Me too!" she breathed. "I have been taken by you." Her hands crawled to his shoulders and held on, like the wind would throw her off her feet. "I cannot even..."

"Mrs. Aldridge is here, lovebirds."

Mary tore away from him at once, her face

turning the reddest of the reds. He chuckled, only quietly, his heart finding solace in her response. *She was taken by him too.* And now, for those very words, he'd fight to the end, the promise of her love bright in his head.

"Aren't there candles here?" Mrs. Aldridge sounded shocked. "You envelope yourselves in dark and do all sort of things?" She shot him a pointed look. "You have me thoroughly awe-bound." She pushed out one of the drawers in the cabinet Mary had previously been scouring through and fetched the candles.

Mary hurried to light them, the amber light brightening the place up a little.

Mrs. Aldridge shot her a look filled with meaning. "We will have a long talk over tea when all of this is over." Her gaze flickered to Will's side for a minute, her gaze stern. "You too."

Will nodded; a small smile on his face. "I shall gladly oblige."

She eyed him warily before continuing, her gaze steady and sure. "Now, we will plan the next course of action."

CHAPTER 14

"Come in."

Mary frowned when Mrs. Aldridge clapped her hands, her gaze wandering to the door.

The door creaked gently and surely, someone walked in, filling the air with the scent of damp earth. But what really unsettled her was the tension that buzzed in the air. The stranger, this elusive man who had appeared from the shadows stood just inside the doorway, his presence like a heavy, unspoken promise.

Will's eyes remained fixed on him, wary but not unyielding.

Mrs. Aldridge didn't waste any more second. "He's going to help us on the next move."

"We have to act fast," the man said, his voice

smooth but carrying an underlying urgency, as though time were slipping through his fingers. "I know you're in deep, and I know Pembroke's game better than anyone."

Mary couldn't quite trust him—her instincts screamed that he was too calm, too composed for someone offering such dangerous information. Will, however, was already leaning forward, his mind working through the possibilities. They needed answers, and if this man truly had them...

"Why are you choosing to help us?" Will's voice cut through the silence like a blade.

"Listen, boy, I know this man."

Will shook his head at Mrs. Aldridge. "You do. We don't." He shook his head. "As far as we are concerned, he was once friends with Pembroke. We all know how that man thinks. How can we be sure he's no different?

The stranger's eyes flickered between Will and Mrs Aldridge, his expression unreadable. "I want nothing but to see Pembroke's empire fall," he replied, though there was a note of hesitation that Mary didn't miss. "I know how it works, how it operates. The corrupt officials, the hitmen, the people he's used—and discarded—along the way."

Mary exchanged a glance with Will, her brow

furrowed. "Why are you telling us this?" she asked, her voice low, almost too cautious.

He leaned forward, his hands clasped in front of him, as though weighed down by the truth he carried. "Because I can get you to Pembroke's empire." He allowed his words to sink in before he continued. "I can give you the chance to wield the weapon you have."

Will's expression hardened. "At what cost?" he asked bluntly.

The stranger's lips curled into a brief, tight smile. "The cost is always high when it comes to him. But if you're willing to pay it…you'll have the chance to destroy him."

The air between them grew thick with unspoken questions as the stranger's words hung heavily in the room. "What exactly are you offering?" Mary finally asked, her voice laced with wariness.

"The full picture," the man replied. "The story you've been piecing together with your little crusade. Pembroke's reach goes far beyond the docks and the political theatre you've seen so far. He controls the magistrates, the officers, and even the higher-ups in the city's underworld. I know his every move, the people he trusts, the ones who've fallen into his pocket."

THE MATCH GIRL

Will's hands tightened into fists. "What does that mean for us?"

The stranger's eyes glimmered darkly. "It means you've been playing a dangerous game without knowing all the rules. Pembroke isn't just a name. He's a shadow that stretches across this city. If you continue without the full truth, you're just marching into his trap."

"You're only saying the same things," Tommy muttered, an irritated look on his face. "Tell us what you know if you really want to help. Besides, why come out now?" Tommy stepped out of the shadows. "You reek of ulterior motives!"

"I've been waiting," he replied, his voice firm. "Waiting for the right moment to approach you. You've stirred the pot, and now I'm offering to show you the recipe."

He glanced toward the window, the faint echo of approaching footsteps muffling his words. "You can't win without the whole picture, and you need my help to see it through."

Mary wasn't sure if she hated him more for the mystery he brought with him or the fact that he seemed to know everything about them—everything about their struggle. Will looked at the stranger with a sharp, calculating gaze.

"You still haven't told us who you are," Will pressed. "We've been chasing ghosts long enough. Who are you, really?"

"I told you. I know him." Mrs. Aldridge, who had been quiet all along said, a bored look on her face. "He means no harm."

The stranger's face tightened. "I am Blackstone," he asked, almost with disdain. "I'm someone from Pembroke's past—a shadow he thought long gone. And now I'm here. That's all you need to know."

The air grew even colder at his cryptic reply. Mary crossed her arms, unconvinced. "But why should we trust you? For all we know, you could be playing us."

He didn't flinch. "You don't have to trust me," he said. "But you'll soon have no choice. You're in this whether you like it or not."

His words hit hard, leaving Mary speechless. He was offering them a way out, a chance to bring down Pembroke—but the cost would be immense. Could they trust him? Could they trust anyone?

"We need to think about this," Tommy said, his voice steady but edged with a trace of doubt.

Mary nodded, torn. Blackstone's offer was tantalizing—everything they had worked for could come to fruition. But the fear gnawed at her. The fear that they might be walking into an even darker pit. "I don't know," she murmured. "It feels wrong. All of this."

Will turned to her, his gaze softened. "I know. But if we don't act now, we'll lose everything."

The man stepped forward, his eyes locked on Mary. "If you trust me, you'll have the truth and win. But if you don't, you'll never know the full extent of Pembroke's hold on this city. It's your call."

Mary's heart pounded in her chest. She wanted to trust Will, to believe that they could beat Pembroke. But she also knew that the truth came at a cost—one they might not be able to pay.

Just as the weight of the decision hung heavy in the air, the sound of approaching footsteps reached their ears. The subtle scrape of boots against cobblestones. The thud of men moving in tandem.

Will and Mary exchanged a quick glance. They had no time to debate anymore.

"Get ready," Blackstone hissed. "They're here."

"Bless my soul," Tommy groaned.

The door slammed open, and a squad of constables poured in, their eyes sharp, their hands poised around their weapons. Behind them stood Pembroke, his face a mask of cold fury.

He smiled coldly as his gaze swept over the trio.

"I told you I would return," he said softly. "But now, it seems I must deal with you more personally."

Mary could feel her heart pound. Blackstone had somehow vanished in the midst of it all.

"Come on!"

She jumped, only to see Mrs. Aldridge behind her, pulling back a door from—

What?!

Did every building have such hidden doors and passageways?

Blackstone pulled her into the dark passage, his voice sharp. "Through here."

They ducked through a narrow alleyway, the sound of chasing feet growing louder behind them. Every corner they turned seemed to bring them closer to being trapped, but the stranger seemed to know where to go. His movements were fluid, practiced, as though he had been running these streets for years.

They ran through the back streets, passing darkened buildings and alleyways that seemed to close in on them. The distant shouts of the constables echoed behind them.

They reached an abandoned building, its silhouette dark against the night sky. Blackstone turned to them, his face unreadable, his eyes burning with a mixture of urgency and resolve.

"You've made it this far," he said, his voice low and measured. "But now comes the true test. You've seen how far Pembroke's reach goes. How deep his corruption runs. The choice is yours. Join me, and you'll learn everything. Or you can continue this futile game on your own, and I can promise you—no one wins."

Behind them, the faint whistle of approaching constables grew louder. Will and Mary stood, frozen, the weight of the decision crushing them.

"Make your choice," he said.

The distant sound of footsteps drew nearer.

"Let's do this!"

Mary and Will looked back at Tommy, their eyes wide with shock.

He shrugged. "For now, we flow with the tides."

CHAPTER 15

With the ledger already circulating, Blackstone's records and the signed ledger gave the reformists something undeniable—a solid proof of theft, illegal executions, bribes to the crown, and secret payments made to silence orphans' deaths at the factories.

That morning, they all made their way to the courthouse at dawn, escorted by a growing crowd of supporters. Word had spread as more copies of the exposé had been printed overnight by an underground press. The streets buzzed with unrest and hope.

And fear.

No one knew what Pembroke would do next.

At the steps of the courthouse, Pembroke was

already there, surrounded by armed guards, the magistrate flushed with fury.

"You dare bring this circus here?" he barked. "You think the law will side with liars and children?"

Will stepped forward, his voice steady. "No. We think the law will side with the truth."

He handed the documents to a robed official who had just emerged from the building, flanked by press and witnesses. There was no going back.

The official took one look at the signatures, the records, and raised his hand.

"We will convene immediately. And until such time as judgment is passed… Magistrate Pembroke, you are hereby suspended."

The crowd exploded. Some in cheers. Others in angry, boiling cries of justice. Pembroke surged forward, but Will was there in a flash, hand pressed to his chest.

"Try it," Will hissed, "and see how fast this crowd turns on you."

Pembroke's face, red with humiliation, contorted as constables he once commanded stepped in and placed iron cuffs on his wrists. The man shrieked like a wounded animal, protesting innocence, calling them traitors.

Will didn't hear the rest. His knees suddenly felt

weak, not with fear, but with something like release. After everything, the running, the hiding, the nights without sleep they had done it.

Pembroke was falling. And they had pushed.

"We did it!"

This time, Mary embraced him, her arms wound tight around his neck. "We did it!"

That evening, the city was quieter than it had been in months. Word had travelled fast. Pembroke would stand trial. The crown, embarrassed by the proof of its local corruption, had sent word of a commission to investigate the entire city's chain of command.

Aldridge was already preparing a new press. Tommy had gone to find Father O'Malley to deliver the news. Even Blackstone, once feared, had found a strange peace as he promised to testify against the man he once served.

And Mary? Mary found herself beneath the lantern light outside the orphanage, her breath visible in the chill, her heart unsteady for the first time not from fear, but from something far softer.

Will stood beside her, quiet. Always steady. Always there.

"You didn't say much during the tribunal," she said at last.

He turned to her. "Didn't need to. You said it all."

She laughed softly. "Do you always have to be so noble?"

"No," he said, voice low. "I don't have to. But I want to be. For you."

She looked up at him, that familiar smirk on his lips softened by something raw. Something real.

"Mary," he whispered. "I've loved you since the moment you burned your hands shoving kindling into a furnace you couldn't afford to fix." He held her hand gently. "You made all of this happen. You led me to Father O'Malley, Mrs. Aldridge and Tommy. You saved my life."

Tears slipped down her cheeks before she could stop them.

"Did I tell you?" She sniffed. "I'm scared, Will...of the future, of us, of everything."

"I know," he said. "Me too."

"But I love you." Her words came out shaky, but true. "I love how stubborn you can be. I love your tenacity, your drive... everything." She chuckled, the tears still in her eyes. "I almost feel bewitched."

Will stepped closer. He reached for her hands, held them with reverence. "Then stay. Let's rebuild this city together. Let's write it in ink and fire."

Mary leaned into him, and their foreheads touched. "You mean it?"

"I've never meant anything more in my life."

The kiss was soft at first. A quiet promise. Only that soon, it deepened... sweet, urgent, and whole. Not just passion...but something older and stronger.

A vow made between bruised hearts that still dared to beat.

EPILOGUE

A Few Weeks Later

The press spun again, and this time not with rebellion, but with stories of rebuilding. The city was changing. Slowly, but surely. Mary now wrote under her own name. Will opened a new shop, with a reading room in the back for children who couldn't afford school.

Tommy visited often. Father O'Malley helped the commission root out corruption across the port. Mrs. Aldridge started her own paper, a righteous and stubborn thing she proudly called The Morning Reckoning.

And Will and Mary?

They shared a small flat above the orphanage, with ivy growing across the windows and laughter that drifted down to the street below. At night, he read her the stories she used to dream of writing. She kissed the ink off his fingers when he stayed up drawing designs for a new press.

They had found not just love, but freedom. Together.

And for the first time in a long, brutal while, the match girl's fire was no longer a desperate spark in the dark.

It was a flame.

A guiding light.

Forever.

ALSO BY BEATRICE WYNN

A Rag Pickers Promise

A compelling tale of hope, courage, and survival in Victorian London.

In the unforgiving streets of Victorian London, young ragpicker Eliza Tate fights to care for her fragile younger brother, Harry. With their lives overshadowed by spiralling debts and the threat of eviction, Eliza takes desperate risks at the perilous docks, determined to protect their small, precious refuge.

Her life takes an unexpected turn when she meets Jonah Quinn, a guarded dockworker with a troubled past he longs to forget. Despite his own battles, Jonah finds himself drawn into Eliza's struggle against poverty, exploitation, and ruthless creditors. Together, they forge an unlikely alliance, testing their courage, trust, and hearts.

As danger escalates, can Eliza and Jonah overcome the powerful forces determined to crush their hope, or will their fragile dreams vanish beneath London's harsh reality?

A Ragpicker's Promise is a stirring narrative of resilience, redemption, and the extraordinary strength found within unexpected bonds.

DOWNLOAD NOW